JODIE A.
SAMUEL

Suzie's *Gift*

novum pro

© 2024 novum publishing

ISBN 978-3-99131-934-4
Editing: Chris Beale
Cover photos: Nexusplexus,
Inna Tarnavska | Dreamstime.com
Cover design, layout & typesetting:
novum publishing

www.novum-publishing.co.uk

The jacket lay on the ground beside her, as she sat with her back against the wall; her hand to her chest, feeling her heartbeat slowing with each gulping breath.

That time it had seemed so real – but how could it be?

The man had been there, his lined face leering over her for just a moment before he was gone.

She'd seen him before. Today. Here!

The urgency began to set in as she struggled to stand. She had to get help, now. Before it was too late.

1

Both mobiles went off together.

'Hi,' chimed Melissa, at exactly the same time as Suzie reached for her own phone and uttered the same greeting.

Suzie and Melissa were in their local café; it was only 6.10pm but already it sounded like the guys had had a drink. Melissa was on the phone to Max, while Suzie spoke to Simon. The four of them had been friends since primary school and now, at eighteen, were all excited about their forthcoming year at university. Despite the years that had passed, all four still got on really well; they even still vetted each other's girlfriends and boyfriends – not that anything serious had ever developed.

'Oh, my God! You're kidding,' said Suzie at the same time as Melissa started laughing down the phone at Max. At that exact moment, as if on cue, both Simon and Max walked into the same café the girls were in and greeted them with big grins on their faces. Melissa jumped up and screeched.

'£48,000! You?' causing the customers around them to turn their way and frown at the commotion.

'Yes,' said Max, unable to lose his wide grin as the girls shushed each other and settled back down. 'Can you believe that it's all down to our Suzie here?' he continued, sitting down next to Suzie and putting his arm round her.

Max suited Suzie; with his blond hair and blue eyes, he was a good 6' tall. Everyone thought they were a good match, with her brunette, shoulder-length hair, big brown eyes, and gorgeous figure, complemented by an olive complexion. They would have been the perfect couple. Not in their eyes though – it was never going to happen.

Simon and Melissa were totally different by comparison. Simon, 5'8", had black hair, green eyes, and a hot temper; whereas Melissa had lovely auburn hair, only 5'3" and had a white complexion that looked more suited to an albino rabbit.

'You remember that night last September when we decided to do the Ouija board?' said Simon.

Melissa interrupted him, 'You mean *you* decided to do the Ouija board. And even then, it was only after you knew about Suzie!'

'Yes, yes, okay then. Not that it really matters whose idea it was! All that matters is that it worked.'

'What worked?' said Suzie. 'All I remember is you two boys acting about. You asked about ghosts, spirits, and football. I mean, honestly, you're like a stuck record sometimes! Do you ever think about anything else?'

'That's just it; we asked the Ouija board loads of serious stuff, and then at the end, before we finished, we asked it who was going to win the football Premiership.'

'Yes,' said Suzie, nodding. 'And then you thought I'd made it all up. In fact, I seem to recall you referred to the answer I gave as "absurd"!'

'Yes, well, good job I didn't go on my instincts and went with what Simon said.'

'What are you talking about?' said Melissa.

'Well, the board spelt out that Derby would win the Premiership, but considering they'd only just moved up from the Championship the previous season by play-offs, there seemed absolutely no way they were going to win the Premiership,' said Max.

'Well, we thought you were messing about, but then Simon here said, "What the hell! Let's put £25.00 on Derby to win." And that was it.

I'm not saying we forgot about the bet we put on. We just didn't think much else about it. We always thought it was the worst £25.00 we ever spent,' shrugged Max.

'Then suddenly time had passed. Derby was in eighth place, and it hit us that they may actually have a chance,' butted in Simon, earning a light shove from his friend.

'I can't believe you didn't tell us,' grumbled Suzie, clearly outraged. 'We could have had fun keeping an eye on them as well. Better still, we could have put a bet on them ourselves.'

'I know,' said Simon. 'I must admit it's been pretty intense these last few months, especially when it looked more and more like they were really in with a chance.'

'The crunch came when they reached fourth place, and there were only three games left to play,' cut in Max, continuing his story. 'To cut a long story short, there were only six points between Derby and Chelsea…'

'Can you just get to the point?' said Suzie, her disgruntlement easing away as the boys' mood became infectious.

'You jammy gits!' exploded Melissa, as the boys whispered in hushed tones that they had, just that afternoon, found out that Derby had taken the Premiership title. 'How much again?'

'Well, we've got to go see the bookies on Monday, but we reckon about £48,000.'

All four stared at each other for a second and then burst out laughing. Attracting the unwanted gazes of their neighbouring customers for the second time in the last few minutes, Suzie put a hand on Max's arm and squeezed it.

'Can you imagine what you can do with that money?' said Suzie.

'Honestly, we've done nothing else. But let's face it, without Suzie we wouldn't have put the bet on in the first place,' said Max, Simon nodding in agreement. 'Half of it is yours.'

2

Monday morning came around and the long-awaited visit to the bookies brought even more good news. It wasn't £48,000 as first thought, but an incredible £58,600. The guys went straight round to Suzie's, where both girls were sat catching up on their favourite TV show.

'Oh my God,' said Melissa slowly, while Suzie stared at the cheque in disbelief. 'What are you going to do now? Have you given it any more thought?'

'Well, like we said on Saturday, the first thing we're going to do is share it with you two, especially you, Suzie. After the year you've had, at least something good has come out of it,' said Max knowingly.

Suzie turned away a little, trying to hide the pained look that she knew would only result in fresh waves of sympathy and awkwardness.

'The family is at peace; I don't need money to remind me of that.'

'Yes, I didn't mean that, Suze, sorry, I just meant with the stress you were under...' Max tailed off, feeling awful. He really hadn't meant to put it like that. In fact, he didn't really know what to say to her at all about what she'd been through. How could he when he didn't really understand it himself?

'It's okay. I know what you meant. And anyway, I got through it, didn't I?'

'You've got to laugh, haven't you?' said Simon, turning to Max and digging his elbow into his friend's ribs as they once again started reeling off ways to spend their windfall.

Simon always was the one to diffuse an awkward conversation, and Suzie found herself thankful for the change in topic. As her friends carried on discussing their big win, her mind wandered, just for a moment, to the family she had become so close to and what they had lost.

'Remember the guy who took our money off us when we put the bet on?'

Suzie snapped back to the present as the face of the pale girl faded once again from her mind.

'He all but laughed in our faces,' continued Simon, 'telling us we might as well just give him the £25.00 and let him keep it for us. You know, it's a pity he wasn't still working there today when we picked up the cheque – we could have given him £25.00 as a tip.'

At that moment, Suzie's Mum, Jill, walked into the kitchen where all four were seated. 'I thought I heard voices.' She smiled, looking over at the boys. Jill had known Max and Simon since they were just three-foot-tall; always stopping by her house in search of snacks or a play-date with her daughter and her friend – or, as was often the case, both.

'Yes, great thanks, Mrs. Lloyd,' chimed the boys, earning themselves a smile and a mock-stern nod from Jill.

'You know to call me Jill, boys. I've known you how long?' She knew they'd never change, and she loved them for it, but Mrs. Lloyd felt so formal that sometimes she couldn't help herself.

As she put on her coat and gave her daughter a quick kiss on the cheek, Jill could tell there was something in the air. Something the teenagers weren't telling her – but she knew better than to pry.

'We should all decide what we want to spend it on,' said Max once the door had closed behind Jill. 'We've worked it out, and it comes to £29,300 for you two, and the same for us boys. Not bad, eh?'

Suzie was quiet while Max, Simon and Melissa began contemplating what they were going to do next. Max and Simon wanted to spend their share on a gap year travelling around Europe – something they had been talking about and fantasising about since the group was fourteen years old and had just come back from their first school trip in Belgium. Melissa's plan was far simpler: spend, spend, spend…

'Come on, Suzie,' probed Max, bringing her back to the present. 'What about you? Any grand plans or ideas?'

'What, sorry hhmm – no, not really. After what's happened lately, I think I'm going to keep it aside and use it for travelling expenses. Maybe work with the police like they want me to.'

'Are you seriously going to do it then? Work for the police?' asked Simon carefully. 'That'd be pretty cool.'

Suzie nodded slowly. 'Oh yes, I've thought about it quite a lot and it scares me, but I think I've got to do it. I'm not sure I have a choice!'

All three of them agreed with Suzie. After all, she'd been on one hell of a journey, and they were nothing if not loyal to her decision.

⊙⊙⊙

They've taken me into a separate room now; told me I have to tell them who it was I saw. I think they're pulling together some photos, I'm not sure yet. Bernard said it wouldn't be too much longer, but I'm so thirsty, and I've been in this room for ages.

I'm not sure if they believe me – Bernard said he'd look after me and make sure I wasn't on my own, but what if the man sees me? I don't yet understand what I saw, but I'm starting to realise that it might be a bit more serious than I thought.

It was like the jacket was showing me something. Okay, I know that sounds ridiculous, utterly absurd, but I don't know what else to say. You know the phrase 'if walls could talk...' – well, what if THINGS could talk?

What would they say? What can they see?

Am I going mad?

3

As she got ready for bed that night, Suzie let her mind run back over the day's events. The boys' win, the conversations about how they'd spend their money; Max's comments about her experience the summer before…

He was right. The last twelve months had been virtually unforgettable, and she was still learning how to deal with it. It was always there, and she knew now that she could handle it – but that didn't mean she understood what it was or why it was there.

She knew now, after giving herself plenty of time to think about it, that working with the police was definitely what she wanted to do. She wanted to help, and she knew that she had the power to do just that. What had happened to her was bizarre and unlikely to ever completely make sense, but what did that matter? Over the last few months, Suzie had received so many letters from people not just locally, not just in the UK, but worldwide. People who wanted her to help them. She'd opened a few of the letters, but after the upset of reading them, decided to leave the rest for a while. One day soon, very soon, she would have the guts to open them all, but for now she knew she had to take it one step at a time.

Returning to Epping was the one step she wasn't yet ready for. But no matter how hard she tried to make plans and occupy her free weekends, she knew she couldn't avoid it forever.

4

Jill had been brought up in Epping, only leaving the town when she'd met Suzie's Dad, Eddie. Eddie was a brickie and worked all over Britain – he lived on the road, going where the job took him. It was on one of these jobs working on a new housing estate near Jill's home that they met.

It had been a classic case of love at first sight, and she dropped everything to follow him around the country; marrying him within a couple of years and welcoming their first child a mere twelve months later.

Suzie didn't remember a great deal about her childhood – but she did recall that it had felt perfect. Until she was seven, walking home from school with her friend and friend's mum and walking through the red front door into a world she didn't recognise, that is.

A world where her dad was gone.

Eddie had been killed in a car accident on his way home from work. Suzie knew everything there was to know about the accident, but really, most of that came from the articles she had slaved over as a teenager, rather than her memories. Now, that day felt like a story from someone else's life, something she read about in the paper, or maybe from a movie she saw as a child. It wasn't her life. Eddie was a happy but increasingly distant memory now, and Jill was the only steady thing in her life.

Jill and their new life in Leeds. Yet, despite being so settled and so happy, they would still go back to Jill's hometown in Epping to visit Jill's mother – Suzie's Grandmother – Rose, every few months.

Rose was what her local neighbours called a 'sweet older woman', caught up in her own life but all too happy to offer an opinion on yours if asked. Going down to Epping was nice, but it never failed to bring up painful memories for Suzie, and she often found herself just staying in, sitting with her mum and her grandma and swapping tales and stories from their day-to-day lives.

Little did she know that spending time at Grandma's was about to get a whole lot more interesting.

His face was lined and rugged, weather spots marking his cheeks and a cruel glint in his eye that I couldn't get out of my mind. His greying brown hair was hidden under a beanie hat, but I spotted a few tufts sticking out around his neck. I always was perceptive.

They made me look at the photo for what felt like hours, but could only have been a few seconds before I nodded and turned away. I'm on my own now, waiting to be told what to do next. They wouldn't let Bernard in with me, and the look on his face as I walked into the windowless room was nothing short of pitiful. I wonder what he's doing now; whether they're quizzing him too?
He doesn't understand this any more than I do. I saw this man – and yet how can I have? I wasn't there. Was I?

The police don't get it; they think I'm mad. Just the mad admin assistant trying to make a name for herself; that's what they'll all be saying. But something I said must make sense; otherwise, why would they be listening?

The jacket sits in the evidence room now, safe and sound in a clear plastic bag and ready to be sent off for evidence. I feel a stab of something that seems a little like jealousy. What I'd do to be back; safe in my evidence room away from all this trouble.

5

Twelve months earlier...

The journey from Leeds to London passed by without incident, and pretty soon the girls were stretching their legs and prodding Jill awake. She had fallen asleep listening to her audio book, and while the girls clearly found it quite amusing, she herself felt a slight wave of irritation at herself for allowing her mind to switch off for so long, missing goodness knows how many pages and chapters. Where on earth had she dropped off, and how was she going to work out what she had missed?

She shook off her irritation as they stepped off the train into the cooler air – she hadn't realised how stuffy it had been on the train, no wonder she'd fallen asleep – and saw her mother, Rose, waving from behind the ticket barrier.

As Jill caught up to Suzie and Melissa, Rose's face broke into a grin. "Suzie, my love, you've grown! And Melissa, it's so wonderful to see you again!" Then, as she turned to Jill, "Hello, love," with a smile.

Jill allowed herself to be enveloped in her mother's hug while the girls picked up their bags and broke away, chattering and pointing towards the recently opened Harry Potter shop with excitement.

When Melissa and Suzie had asked Jill if Melissa could join them for a few days in London, she hadn't hesitated to agree. After years growing up around Epping Forest and the surrounding neighbourhoods, she knew how much there was to explore and enjoy; bittersweet memories that constantly reminded her of the fact that Suzie was growing up and experiencing her life without the joy that siblings could bring. Losing her husband the way she had, Jill had long since given up on ever having another child, and now, with her daughter fast approaching her twenties, she knew that the friendships she held dear were really the only siblings she needed.

While Jill's head was caught in the past for those few short moments, Suzie and Melissa were very much in the present, planning day trips to London, nights out in Epping, and all the walks they wanted to do while they were "down South" – as Melissa put it.

Rose looked on happily. She had met Melissa on quite a few occasions over the years while staying up in Leeds, and she liked her. The two girls were good for each other, and Rose knew that Jill was happy that Suzie had found someone she felt as close to as she might a sister. Even now, as she glanced at her daughter while they made their way out to the car, Rose could see she was deep in thought, but knew better than to disturb her daughter's train of thinking. The loss of Eddie had hit them all hard, but Jill had never really gotten over it. How could she?

Jill's mind was brought back to the present as they arrived at Rose's jeep. A blazing orange colour that her mum described as "jazzy", Jill chuckled as Melissa pointed towards the car in amazement, and Suzie popped open the boot with a laugh.

'Grandma always has been ahead of her time!' she said through her laugh. Rose winked at her.

The two of them had always been close, despite the vast generation gap, and Jill knew that at some point over the next few days, her mum would take Suzie aside to do their usual – catch up, have a gossip, and exchange any worries that Suzie didn't feel like she wanted to tell her mum. It was the same every time they visited, and Jill found that, actually, she was glad that her mum and her daughter had such a close relationship. With it just being the two of them so much of the time, knowing someone else cared about Suzie as much as she did was sometimes all she needed to feel safe.

☉☉☉

By the time they pulled into Rose's drive, Jill was ready for a little peace and quiet. The girls hadn't stopped laughing and pointing out the window for the entire journey, noting the various sights and road names – and even a group of boys they must have found attractive, given the lowered voices and giggles. Jill needed a cup of tea.

It was already 3.30pm, and no sooner had they got through the door than Rose was putting the kettle on. In a whirlwind of long hair, teenage perfume and summer dresses, Suzie and Melissa shot past Jill, dropped their bags in the guest bedroom, and turned back towards the front door.

'Just taking Melissa down to the Mall and Town Street,' said Suzie, kissing her mum on the cheek and giving her grandma a quick wave.

'We'll be back soon, but I've got my mobile with me if you need us for anything!' she called as the door closed behind them.

Peace at last.

As Rose bustled around the kitchen making tea and organising stuff for dinner, Jill moved up the stairs to unpack, pausing for a moment before she opened the door to her old bedroom and took in the familiar surroundings. Still her room; the same bay window overlooking the garden, framed by pale cream curtains dotted with small flowers. The only difference now was that instead of her posters displaying the Bay City Rollers and Starsky and Hutch, there was now a subtle hint of lemon wallpaper, candles and white-framed pictures of delicate flowers. Her room – but from a lifetime ago.

As Jill went back downstairs and into the living room, she saw Rose had finished in the kitchen and now sat surrounded by bags of clothes. Rose often did this – stocking up on charity shop goodies for her and Suzie to try – and Jill always found herself immensely grateful for her mother's generosity. It was easy to forget to buy new clothes for herself, and she knew that Suzie's taste in fashion was always dipping in and out of various trends and styles. Keeping up with it required a full-time job and extra income, and without Rose's frequent charity shop splurges, Jill knew that Suzie would soon become tired and disinterested in whatever already sat in her wardrobe at home.

Rose showed Jill what she'd bought. Knowing Suzie was interested in becoming a fashion designer one day, she knew that a good pattern or unique fabric was more important than an accurate fit, and that if her granddaughter didn't like what she pulled out of the bag, she was sure to turn it into something fabulous!

Rose and Jill were just finishing their second cup of tea and opening the third bag of clothes when the girls arrived home. With a rush of laughing and cheery voices, they ran straight upstairs to unpack their bags, reliving stories of the things they had seen on their short trip to stake out the Mall.

The room the girls were to sleep in was at the back of the house, overlooking the woods in the distance. Rose had put two single beds in there when Suzie was small, as she had wanted to stay in the same room as her mum, and the beds had never moved since. Rose looked forward to her visitors, and liked to keep the room exactly as they might expect it, should they choose to turn up to see her any day. Goodness knows they were always welcome.

Her husband, Philip, had died a mere five years earlier, but with the loneliness that she now faced most days, it felt like longer. They were all devastated when he'd suffered the fatal heart attack, but the loss no doubt hit Suzie the hardest. While Rose and Jill felt a slither of gratitude that his short-lived suffering was at least now over, for poor Suzie, the loss of her grandad simply became an unbearable reminder of when her dad had died, and it had taken her a long time to move forward.

Much like with her grandma, Suzie was close to Philip, and he played true to the role, spending copious amounts of time with his granddaughter whenever she came to visit. Rose smiled as she remembered his dark grey head of hair, flecked with white but still going strong – even as his brother – her brother-in-law – slowly turned completely bald. Whenever Philip smiled, it seemed to reach from ear to ear, and his laugh could fill a room tenfold. Everyone loved him – he truly was one of those people that would do anything for anyone.

Since his passing, Jill and Suzie had tried hard over the years to convince Rose to go and live with them, but she wouldn't budge. Rose and Philip had been in Epping since they first married, and she wasn't going to give that up for anything in the world. Not even more time with her family. Epping was their home, and leaving just wouldn't feel right. And after all, Jill had to respect her mum for that – it's exactly what she did herself, too.

6

As Suzie led her friend up the stairs and through the house she thought of as her second home, she found herself regarding the walls and décor as if with a fresh set of eyes. The old-school charm she had once seen was slowly being replaced with a dire need for some tender love and care, and Suzie felt her eyes drawn to cracks in the ceiling and pieces of peeling wallpaper. There was no doubt about it, the house needed a good lick of paint – or six – but it still felt like home, and Suzie was happy to be there.

As she opened the door to her and Melissa's bedroom, she smiled as she spotted the knitted square quilted blanket her grandma had made for her many years ago, bringing back happy – if slightly eerie – memories of the good times gone by. Suzie had faced a lot of loss in her life so far, but she also had some wonderful memories, and she knew deep down that she was lucky.

After unpacking their bags, the girls headed downstairs to finally join Jill and Rose, who had by now finished going through and re-bagging the charity shop clothes. As she popped the kettle on for yet another round of tea, Rose pointed out the bags to Suzie and said she was welcome to pick and choose whatever she wanted.

'There might even be something in there for you too, Melissa. There's no way any of it will fit me anymore!' she chuckled as she set the kettle down on the stove.

The girls settled down on the retro carpet that covered the living room floor and tipped the bags out one by one – earning exasperated looks from Jill and Rose, who had just spent a good half an hour sorting everything back into bags. A scrap of lilac material caught Melissa's eye, and she held it against herself, eliciting a new fit of giggles from Suzie as she tried to work out how it went on. Eventually realising the top was designed to sit on one shoulder, Melissa regarded the item before handing it to Suzie.

'This one's for you. You've got the shoulders for it.'

It looked brand new and was obviously a one-off design; even the label gave nothing away, simply stating "RANDOM" in block capitals.

'Wow, Gran, you've done really well with all these,' said Suzie, as she dug out a knitted dress that was the perfect colour to match Melissa's hair and handed it to her friend.

Rose nodded eagerly. 'Yes, love, I know. Did you know that they even get celebrity clothes in sometimes? For all we know, some of that could have been worn by Lady Gaga – or maybe royalty!'

The girls laughed. 'Yes, Mum, I hear the Royal Family particularly enjoy a trip to Epping,' chuckled Jill as she too started rifling through the piles of clothes once again, drawn in by the enthusiasm of the two girls.

After scanning the piles and identifying one or two items that Rose insisted could well have come from the closet of Lady Gaga – 'or that other singer, Pink is it?' – they ended up with a pile of keepers, a pile of "to be redesigned", and a pile to take back to the shop.

It was only as they carried the final garments upstairs to the girls' room that they realised they were all hungry, having not eaten since breakfast – hours ago! They had been so wrapped up in discovering clothes from the past and discussing the types of people who might have once owned them, that they had completely forgotten their stomachs.

The girls decided, once dinner was over, to stay in that night and go out the next night, carefully planning a route back down to the Mall and Town Street – which may have been only three streets away from Rose's house, but still passed by at least three decent pubs and bars where the girls could show off their new outfits and maybe meet some new people.

Though the night was young, the journey from Leeds had exhausted the girls, and not long after dinner they excused themselves and headed back up the stairs, desperate to try on their new clothes once again and start pulling together some killer outfits for the following night.

◉◉◉

They've told me there was no clear motive.

"Wrong place at the wrong time," one policeman said, as he led me out of the interview room and towards the staff room. "We're investigating what you said, but we can't let you leave. Not yet."

So, they do believe me. I must admit, part of me feels relieved not to be classed as insane – but a bigger part of me is trying hard not to acknowledge the edge in his voice. Why don't they want me to leave? Do they think I might be in danger now because of what I saw?

I know the staff room well; I do work here, after all. But the policeman still leads me all the way to the door and points out the coffee machine before backing away and hurrying off, speaking into his radio fast. I catch odd words as he retreats down the corridor – "search warrant" … "known burglar" … "her life" …

I told them I saw who killed the man in the jacket – the man who, they say, was in the wrong place at the wrong time. The man who did it was here, in the police station, mere hours ago. But he wasn't here for murder – far from it. 'Petty theft', his check-in card said.

If what I saw was true, then he's far more dangerous than any of us realise.

7

It had been a hot day, and the sticky warmth was lasting well into the evening; the August heat penetrated through the old house's walls and windows, turning the girls' bedroom into a sauna. Suzie flung open the windows and flopped down on her bed, although the air from outside did little to stifle the heat that had sat in the room while they all enjoyed their dinner downstairs.

Melissa started working through the piles of clothes again, standing in front of the mirror and holding skirts and dresses out for Suzie to try.

'Your gran's got quite an eye for fashion Suze,' she said as she held a spectacular 70s style dress in front of her and pulled a few poses in the full-length mirror.

Suzie picked out a skirt she'd had her eye on earlier, stepping in front of the mirror to try it for size. Rose had picked a three-quarter-length tight black pencil skirt, which looked like something a receptionist might wear in a Hollywood movie. The skirt was simple, but as she pulled it over her hips, Suzie knew without looking that the skirt suited her slim frame.

'Gran has got pretty good taste. There's no way I would have picked this up myself, but actually, it's pretty cool!' she agreed, fumbling around in her bag and pulling out the diamante sandal heels that she knew would go just perfectly with her new skirt.

'What a look,' nodded Melissa. 'You should wear that on Friday night when we go out. You look fabulous!'

And so it went on; the girls tried different outfits on as the sun continued to set, and the evening wore on – occasionally breaking into fits of giggles when one or other of them came across an item that looked completely ridiculous.

'Oh no, Suzie, look. Your gran's even bought a pair of pyjamas,' said Melissa as she pulled a white flannelled top out of the few clothes they had yet to critique. A few seconds later, she located the matching bottoms and laid them out for Suzie to see, the two girls marvelling at the pyjama set that they seemed to have missed when they first assessed the bags of clothes downstairs.

The pyjamas were white with big pink hearts all over them. The flannel material was soft, and the white of the material was a pure white that could only mean one thing – these pyjamas were new, Melissa felt a wave of melancholy as she realised that they probably hadn't been worn much. Who had donated this pair of girls' pyjamas without hardly wearing them?

◉◉◉

Once they had tried on all the clothes and pulled together a few decent outfits, the girls had got their second wind and decided it was time to leave the stuffy bedroom behind and enjoy what was left of the beautiful summer day. Picking up a wine glass each and pouring out the last of the Prosecco they found abandoned in the kitchen, they wandered outside to find Jill and Rose enjoying a glass as they overlooked the garden, discussing Rose's vegetable patch and her plans to join a beekeeping club in the Autumn months.

'Thank you so much, Gran,' Suzie said as she leaned in and gave her grandma a hug. 'You picked some real gems in that charity shop; I can't wait to get my sewing machine out!'

'Oh love, it was nothing!' replied Rose, beaming at the thrill of it all. 'To be honest with you, I got quite a buzz – especially when they said some of the clothes were from celebrities! You should go yourself while you're both down here. They said they get new stock in pretty much every day!'

'We did have one question, though,' piped up Melissa as the girls settled on the grass next to the adults. 'There was a pair of pyjamas in one of the bags. They look brand new, but I don't think I've ever actually seen pyjamas in a charity shop before. Did the shop assistants in the shop say anything about them?'

'Oh yes, I did mean to mention them. It was weird actually, one of the ladies working in the shop brought them to my attention and was adamant that I buy them. They were only a few pounds and in really good condition and so I thought what the heck. I've washed them since bringing them home, so they should be just grand,' she said heartily before backtracking a little. 'They did only cost a few pounds though, love, so if you don't like them, then I won't mind...!'

'No, no, I really like them,' butted in Suzie quickly. Her grandma had been so good to her she didn't want to up-set her by saying she thought the pyjamas left at a chari-ty shop was a little weird, and anyway they were a pretty design. Besides, all she had with her to wear in bed was a couple of old T-shirts and some shorts – it might be nice to wear a proper matching set for once! 'I think I'll wear them tonight.'

◉◉◉

An hour later, as the girls were getting ready for bed, Melissa had a slightly uneasy feeling in the pit of her stomach. She thought it was a bit weird that Suzie wanted to wear the charity shop pyjamas, but her friend was adamant that she wouldn't upset her grandma, and besides, they were better than what she had with her.

Melissa shrugged to herself and got into bed. It had been a lovely afternoon and evening. She was looking forward to their night out tomorrow, and really – what was the worst that could happen?

8

She awoke with a start, feeling around for her phone so she could see the time and figure out what had woken her up so sharply. The sun shone in her bleary eyes, and she realised it must be later than she first thought.

Seeing that the time was just past 9am, she was about to swing her legs out of bed when she heard a sharp moan coming from the other side of the room. Deep and full of melancholy, the sudden noise had come from Suzie, who Melissa could now see was still sound asleep – though it didn't seem to be a very peaceful slumber. Hurrying over to comfort her clearly distressed friend, Melissa gently shook Suzie until she opened her eyes.

'Suzie? Suze? Are you okay? I think you're having a nightmare. Wake up, it's fine!'

'What time is it?' Suzie asked, putting her arm up to shield her eyes from the sunshine that was radiating through the flimsy curtains.

'It's just after 9am. I think your mum and grandma are already up. Are you okay?' Melissa asked again, concerned that Suzie seemed tense and on edge as she sat up in her bed.

'I probably would have slept all morning if you hadn't woken me up. I feel exhausted,' Suzie admitted. 'I had the most vivid dream ever. I mean, *really* vivid. Horrible, actually.'

She stood up and headed towards the bathroom, Melissa following close behind.

'What about? Was it your dad?' Melissa probed gently, knowing her friend still had the occasional nightmare that took her back to the day her dad had died, with roaring trucks and white sheet-covered bodies.

'No!' replied Suzie sharply. 'I mean, no, this was different. Those dreams are awful, yes, but a part of me always knows it's not real. This felt... really real.'

Melissa waited with bated breath, not wanting to push Suzie, but Suzie simply pushed past her and started down the stairs.

'Let me get my head around it first. I'll tell you over breakfast.'

The two girls went downstairs and into the kitchen, where Rose and Jill were sat with steaming mugs of coffee: a pan of bacon sizzling on the hob. Getting up to fetch them a coffee and load crispy bacon between slices of bread, Jill noted that the girls were unusually quiet, and that Suzie looked really quite pale.

It was warm in the house; maybe she had been too hot to sleep?

It was Rose who finally broke the silence. 'Did you sleep well, girls?'

Suzie looked up. 'I was just about to tell Melissa... I had the most horrible dream. I don't even know if it was a dream, really, it felt so real. Like it was really playing out in front of me, like that play we went to see with school last month.' She nodded at Melissa, who listened intently. 'Except this wasn't funny,' continued Suzie after a pause.

Jill put her arm around her daughter and gave her a quick squeeze. 'It's over now, darling,' she said warmly, but Suzie shook her head. 'I'm not sure it is.'

◉◉◉

I know what they were talking about now; someone finally told me. They've got a search warrant to search the man's house.

According to Bernard, he was brought in for petty crime, but after I saw what I saw and collapsed in the evidence room, they decided to take what I said seriously.

The man's records show that he's been involved in gang crime before, and is a known thief wanted for quite a few crimes. Not that that's anything compared to what I'm accusing him of.

I didn't really think of it like that before now, but that's what I've done, isn't it? Accused him of something. And if I'm right, but he gets away, he might come after me.

Before, I thought staying here was the worst thing they could make me do, but now I realise that sending me out is worse. All I can do now is sit tight and see if they find anything they can use to take him down.

9

Suzie took a deep breath as she worked out how to start. What she'd seen had been so vivid and so real, and yet she wasn't really sure how to put it into words.

'I was in this lovely garden… really pretty, like someone spent lots of time there. I was on my own, or at least I thought I was, but then suddenly there were two elderly people just in front of me. I guess they'd come out of the big house I could see in the distance, surrounded by beautiful gardens. It was strange, the house looked kind of run down, but the gardens were so beautiful and well-kept. It looked a bit mysterious, really.

'Anyway, they came up to greet me, and that's when I realised I must look like someone else, or at least be someone they recognised. They definitely knew me. I thought they might be relations of Dad's,' she admitted, looking towards Jill with an almost hopeful look in her eye.

'I thought, maybe this is an uncle or an aunt who I never really got to know. Maybe it's Dad greeting me as an old man. I don't know,' she shrugged.

'I can remember climbing up two or three steps, coming to a back-patio door that was open and walking inside with them. They were chatting away like I knew them, and then they hugged me and I was leaving again, heading out to a car with two other adults in it – only these two were much younger. More like your age, Mum.

'I assumed we were heading off back to where I lived, and they kept asking me if I'd had a good time at Grandma and Grandad's, so at least I knew who the old people had been.'

'Where did you drive to?' asked Melissa as Suzie paused to catch her breath.

'I honestly don't know. I remember fields and greenery and a small town, but that bit really was more like a dream than anything else. I knew what I was doing, but I can't put my finger on the details, you know?

'So anyway, then we pulled into this drive, up towards a small house; decent garden – nothing on the old people's house though – and super clean inside the house. I mean, really clean.

'This is when it got weird. The guy asked the woman to make him a cup of tea and said he was hungry. She said she just wanted to put the shopping away first, and suddenly it was like something snapped. He stood up abruptly from the kitchen chair he'd sat in causing it fall to the floor with a bang, but he didn't pick it up.

'He was quite tall, butch, unshaven, and he looked dirty... not DIRT dirty but, you know, like he worked on a building site or something. Kind of like those guys Dad used to hang out with, Mum.' She smiled weakly, looking once again at her mother, who looked increasingly concerned.

'I looked around the corner at where the man had stormed off to, and he was settled in this old armchair in front of the TV; a beer can next to him and the remote glued to his hand. He didn't seem to care at all that he'd been so rude!

'And while he was doing that, the woman just stayed in the kitchen making a sandwich like nothing had happened.'

She sniffed, remembering the feeling of defiance that had overcome her at this blatant exploitation of gender roles.

'Maybe I'm being dramatic and over the top,' she continued. 'But honestly, I don't think I've ever had such a vivid dream before. The details... I even remember what cereals they had lined up on a shelf!'

Rose and Melissa nodded, urging Suzie to continue.

Suzie, starting to feel uncomfortable at all the attention, tried to brush it off. 'I'm sure it was nothing, in fact actually, I wish I hadn't mentioned it. I don't even know...' but Jill cut her off, a little more sharply than she had intended.

'Keep going, Suzie.'

Suzie swallowed. 'Okay... well, I headed upstairs. I remember having a bag with me, and I guess I was going up to unpack it.'

'As I came back down the stairs, I could hear the man shouting again, yelling at the woman about something or other; not even bothered that I was there and could obviously hear everything he was saying. It was like he was possessed or something.'

She looked at her mum again, adding gratefully, 'It's not something I've ever experienced at home, thank goodness, so it felt really shocking to overhear such foul language and abuse.

'When I think about it now, it was like I was on the outside looking in, but dressed in the body of someone who was meant to be there. I mean, they'd come to pick me up, and they gave me a drink, so it's not like I was a spirit, you know, invisible or anything. I was someone they knew and expected to be there – if that's possible in a dream, of course.

'Next thing I knew, I was telling the man to stop shouting; to have more respect for the lady and to stop spoiling everything. That's when he smacked me.'

Rose recoiled in horror, and Melissa's hand shot to her mouth to cover a sudden gasp. Suzie could feel tears welling up in her eyes, unsure why but certain now that the dream had really shaken her.

'He just looked so aggressive and really evil. He walked off saying he was sick of both of us, and that's when the woman finally came to me and inspected my face before pulling me into a hug.'

Her voice soft, Suzie looked at Jill as she said, 'I have a strong feeling the lady was my mum, but that man definitely was not my dad. The lady – my mum – started sobbing and sat down heavily at the kitchen table, saying it was time we went away for a few days.

'As the lady packed her bag, I just seemed to stand still, watching it all gone on around me and then we were gone.'

'We walked out through the front door... we didn't use the car, and then the next moment, we were at the old house with the beautiful garden again.

'Some time later, I'm not sure how long, I realised I'd forgotten my phone. I was meant to be seeing a friend, I think, and I heard myself telling the lady that I would go back to pick my phone up on way to my seeing my friend. I told her I wouldn't be back late and that I loved her.

'Then I left, leaving my "mum" with the elderly couple, and heading off back to the house that we'd just left.'

Suzie took a deep breath as Melissa visibly shuddered. She knew the worst bit was coming, and she wasn't sure she could bear to see the looks of confusion and pity that were already emanating from the faces of her friend, her mum and her grandmother. They would all think she was mad – she knew she couldn't bear that. She had to tread carefully with this next bit.

'You know when you're dreaming, and some parts are clear, but some parts are all mixed up, and you can't really keep up with what's going on? Well… this wasn't like that. It really was real, like a film.'

'Anyway, I reached the house, my home, and I knew the man would be there, so I knocked on the door. I don't know why I didn't just walk in. Clearly this was my home, and I had a key; maybe part of me didn't want to interrupt the man and set him off on another rage. I don't know.

'The guy came to the door, and when he saw it was me, he told me to stay away – we weren't welcome there anymore, and he would forward anything that belonged to me and Mum. I said I'd forgotten my mobile and that it was in my bedroom, but it was like the sound of my voice wound him up even more.'

'I could tell he was really angry, so when he didn't let me in, I tried to just push past him. I knew I could be up there and back out again in ten seconds if I was quick, and I really did need my phone. I didn't have time to wait for him to send it on. But he wouldn't let me pass.'

'Then suddenly, I don't know what happened, but something snapped and before I realised it was time to give up and leave, it was too late. I tried squeezing past him in the doorway again, and that's when he grabbed me by my hair and hissed: 'If you want your mobile let's go get it then.'

By this time, Melissa had both hands to her mouth, and Jill was gripping her mug of coffee so tightly it looked like it could snap. Rose, on the other hand, looked pale – almost ill.

'He dragged me upstairs by my hair,' Suzie continued, 'and every time I tried getting out of his grasp, he kicked me back or yanked my hair even harder. I said it before, but it was like he was possessed, like he didn't realise what he was doing. He was so angry and aggressive, and I was terrified. By the time we reached the top of the stairs, I was crying out and pleading with him to stop, but nothing worked.'

'At some point I must have given up, because after that I didn't really know what was going on. It's all a bit hazy from that point. I know we were at the top of the stairs, then outside the bedroom I had thought was mine, and then I saw his face looming over mine – red and snarling.'

'He threw me into the room and told me to get my phone… and that's when I woke up,' she finished.

◉◉◉

They found a knife hidden among a pile of old clothes and a pair of shoes which, the police believe, may have retained a few traces of blood.

I can't believe it – that what I said may have been right. They say the length and design of the blade matches up to what they know about the wound, though the knife is being taken to the mortuary to be examined properly by a pathologist.

I'm in shock. It was Bernard who brought me the news – he sat me down and told me that my information had proved extremely valuable, and that it may well have been the turning point in what was otherwise looking to be an unsolved robbery gone wrong.

The police have taken the man into custody, and they say he is, in fact, a notorious criminal who started as a thief but has been wanted on manslaughter charges for the past few months.

I can't believe I was right. Why was it me that saw him? And how did such a meaningless, inanimate object create such an extraordinary reaction inside me? I didn't know what I was seeing, and yet this whole time, I have known that what I saw was more than just my imagination or a daydream.

What's happening to me?

10

When Suzie finally looked up and made eye contact with her mum, she knew she hadn't been overreacting. The nightmare may have been just that – a nightmare – but that didn't mean it wasn't troubling, and Suzie knew her mum understood how she would be feeling.

It seemed like Rose could barely make eye contact, staring into her coffee mug with a vacant expression, while Melissa jumped up and threw her arms around her friend.

'I think you need to just tell yourself it was a nightmare,' she said through her hug.

'Yes, I just can't shake it off, that's all.'

Jill sat with a pondering look on her face, and Melissa sat back down, clutching her friend's hand. Just as Suzie was about to speak again, however, Rose jumped to her feet and began bustling around with the kettle, muttering about breakfast and things to do.

'What do you think, Grandma?' Suzie asked the back of her grandma's head. Rose stiffened.

'Oh, I don't know, love,' she said with a nervous laugh. 'Probably just an old nightmare. You know, I used to have terrible ones that I was going to fall off a cliff. Have I ever told you? Jill, you used to...'

But Suzie wasn't listening. Her mind was racing, and as her grandma gave another nervous laugh, she knew she wasn't imagining the nervous look in the old woman's eyes. It was a look she hadn't seen before on her grandma's face, and though she couldn't quite place it, she knew her grandma was hiding something.

The thought made her eyes begin to burn, and she fought back tears as she turned towards her mum again. 'You don't think I'm mad, do you, Mum?'

Jill put her hand on her daughter's hand, squeezed and gave her a smile. Just as she was about to speak, Rose turned to them all with a bright smile on her face; the haunted, nervous look now completely gone.

What was going on?

◉◉◉

Later that morning, when breakfast was finished and the dishes were clean, the girls were upstairs getting dressed and planning their day. Melissa had spent the last hour or so googling 'dream visions' on her mobile and had come up with lists of websites that offered everything from spiritual explanations to conspiracy theories and even exorcisms.

'There's one site here,' she said, sitting cross-legged on Suzie's bed while Suzie did her best to ignore her, 'which says there was a girl who saw... wait a minute. Suzie? Take a look at this.'

Suzie sighed and stood up, unconvinced that her dream meant anything at all, let alone that Melissa would be able to find anything out online. As she reached across, Melissa passed her phone to her friend and showed her what she'd found. It was an old newspaper clipping, probably uploaded or scanned in by some old historian who thought people still cared about the obituaries and announcements made decades ago.

Melissa was pointing at a small article in the corner of the page titled "Local Woman Solves Robbery Gone Wrong". The story was brief and uninteresting, clearly written as more of a space filler than anything else. It told of how the woman had seen a robbery in a dream, and subsequently solved a random robbery by implicating both the victim and the culprit in a line up. A short quote accompanied the story, where the woman said it was the most vivid dream she had ever had, quite unlike anything else.

But what hooked Suzie wasn't the text, nor was it the quote or the headline. There was a picture next to the article of a woman who looked more shell-shocked than anything else. The picture was small and faded, and replicated the quality you might expect from the times – all grey and blurry. But the face was clear enough, and as Suzie looked closer, a thought hit her so suddenly that it felt like a physical roadblock.

The face was much younger, and the grainy quality made it hard to make out any distinguishing features, but still, Suzie knew she had seen this face before. Not in one of those nightmares like she had last night, but in real life. Here, in this house.

Suzie jumped up from the bed and ran to the door. 'Grandma!' she called as she hurried to the stairs.

Just as she was about to steamroller her way into the kitchen, Jill appeared at the living room door. 'She went out, said she had some things to do. What's wrong, Suze?'

Suzie felt her energy deflate as she sat down at the bottom of the stairs, then looked up at her mum. 'Mum, where are Grandma's old photos? Melissa was looking online, and she found an article about a girl, years ago, who... well, she... I guess she was kind of like me. She saw stuff, she saw this guy who killed someone, and the police thought it was a robbery, but it wasn't, she saw what happened, and she told them, and then they found who did it. And there was a picture, and I think – no, I KNOW – I've seen the face before. I think I've seen it here. I think Grandma knows her.'

⊙⊙⊙

As they searched the house for Rose's old boxes of photos, Jill pondered her mother's reaction to Suzie's nightmare and her sudden need to leave the house. Could Rose really know more than she was letting on?

Jill knew that Rose would do anything to protect her granddaughter, believing, as she often said, that the young girl had been through more than enough for a lifetime, let alone her eighteen short years.

It took the trio just under an hour to finally unearth the cardboard box of old photos, stacked under Rose's bed alongside an old yoga mat, a hat box with a hat that Jill hadn't seen since her wedding day, and a lot of dust. By the time they pulled the box out and started going through the photos inside, Jill was slightly worried her mother could walk in any minute. What would she say if she returned home and found them rifling through her personal things?

'Here!' Suzie suddenly exclaimed, and all thought of her mother's reaction vanished from Jill's mind as she gazed at the picture Suzie was holding triumphantly.

The photo showed a group of young people, probably in their early to mid-twenties, arms around each other and smiling at the camera. It was a little hard to tell with the low quality of the photo, but it looked like they were in a large field, with bikes lying next to them. They seemed

44

happy, and Jill found herself lost in the image for a few seconds until her daughter spoke again.

'She's the girl from the paper,' she said, pointing and nodding at Melissa, who stared back at her – speechless. Suzie turned the photo over and read the words, faded from time but still just clear enough to read.

"Martha and the gang."

'My great-grandma's name was Martha,' breathed Jill as Suzie began to rummage through the box again. But her hunt was to no avail – there were no more photos of Martha in any of Rose's boxes, and their search quickly ran dry.

Just as they were packing the last of the boxes back under Rose's bed, they heard the front door open. Melissa looked a little nervous, though Suzie already knew what she had to do.

Jumping to her feet, she headed for the stairs; Jill and Melissa close behind; as they all went to join Rose in the kitchen, where she was unpacking bags of food – including a roast chicken for dinner that night. She looked up as they entered, and Suzie could tell from the look on her face that she was steeling herself for their questions. Suzie only hoped this time she wouldn't run away.

She had to find out what Rose knew, and what she wasn't telling her about her great-great-grandmother.

◎◎◎

It's been a few days now, and things have calmed down on the surface. I was finally allowed to leave the station after they had arrested the man for first-degree murder, and I decided to walk home rather than catch the bus. I was desperate for air.

But as soon as I walked in my front door, I felt disconnected from my own home – unsure what to do.

I can't stop thinking about the man's family – the one who died, I mean. I wonder if they know what happened to him, and for a while I considered going back to the station and asking Bernard to take me to see them. I know I can't do anything to make it better, though, and telling them what I saw would only raise more questions.

Witch-hunting is the stuff of myths and fairy tales nowadays, but my mind keeps going there, and I've found myself in the library more than once, looking at drawings of witches being hunted and reading old stories of their trials and deaths.

Is there witchcraft in my blood? Are the ghost stories we always heard about actually real?

11

It took two cups of tea and at least a dozen biscuits before Rose finally gave in and revealed what she knew – and even then, there was frustratingly little she could tell the girls beyond a name and a few light facts that sounded as much like gossip as anything else.

'Martha King, Fulham Police Station. This one says she was an undercover detective who worked the case,' read Melissa, adding another newspaper cutting to the mounting pile. 'Except... that one says she was just a passer-by who actually saw the crime. And THIS one...' she continued, muttering to herself as Suzie also flicked through pages of old papers.

As Rose didn't have a computer or laptop at home the girls had decided to head for the local library rather than use their mobiles. After searching for little under an hour having eventually extracted Martha's full name from Rose. Though having a name made their search marginally easier, the information available was sporadic and often confined to small articles – there was even one paper that featured the story in the "Mystic Melody" column, shedding a spiritual and weirdly magical haze on the story.

Days ago, she would have found all this laughable, but today she found herself solemnly reading the article and, at points, agreeing with it. This was all too weird.

A couple of hours later, they finally hit a breakthrough. Suzie had been on the phone to Jill, updating her on their findings and sharing her frustration at the lack of coverage, when Melissa grabbed her arm and dragged her over to one of the library's ancient computers.

'Look here,' she hissed, keeping an eye on the Librarian who had been over to shush them at least five times in the last hour. 'Martha King, worked part-time at Fulham Police Station in the filing room every Monday, Tuesday and Thursday, until one day when she suddenly disappeared from the records and stopped clocking in. BUT if you look here...' she said, as she clicked a new tab and opened up a different database, '... Martha King remains on the official employee list for the station for another six years.'

Jill got up from the kitchen table and made what felt like her tenth cup of tea today, picking up her mum's mug as she went. After the stress of the morning and Suzie's horrible nightmare, she found herself thinking about what they could all do together that evening to restore a bit of normality.

It had shocked her to learn that her great-grandmother had been involved in police cases. She knew that she had worked as an admin assistant, but any stories or family information that had been shared had always confined Martha to the filing room or – at best – the reception desk. No one had ever mentioned solving cases before.

The girls were due back at any moment, and Jill knew that they'd be full of stories, questions, and their findings from the day. Rose had been quiet that afternoon, frequently lost in thought. Jill still had a feeling that her mum wasn't telling them everything she knew, but she had long given up trying to extract any more information. She was fighting a losing battle.

Rose would open up when she wanted to, and not a moment before.

'Why did you spend so much time with your grandparents, Mum?' she asked as she sat back down and set a fresh mug of tea in front of Rose. It was almost time to break out the wine – goodness knows they needed it after today! – but Jill found making tea comforting and enjoyed the mundane everyday task.

Rose considered the question for a moment, before answering carefully, 'No real reason. There were five of us, and my own mother, your grandmother, used to get quite overwhelmed sometimes. The boys were older and could fend for themselves, but it was a different time back then, especially for girls, and I couldn't go out by myself like they could. Mum was always busy with the baby, so I'd get sent to our grandparents for the day.

'It was okay!' she added hastily. 'I loved it there. I used to get spoilt rotten. And Grandma would tell me these incredible stories about a girl who could see things that no one else could see.'

She smiled at the memory before continuing. 'I thought the girl was made up. I thought it was just a story. Grandma used to tell it with such eloquence and detail, all the little bits of the story fitting together so perfectly, about how the girl would touch something – an object, or an item of clothing – and it would transport her to a different place. Just like magic. Well, that little girl was my hero. She was so brave, so clever. I used to ask her for stories all the time. I thought it all came from my grandma's mind; even when Suzie was younger, I used to wish that I could come up with stories like it.'

As her mum fell quiet again, Jill voiced what she knew they were both thinking: 'It was real, wasn't it? The stories? They were real, and the little girl was Martha – your grandmother.'

Rose nodded solemnly. 'So it would seem.' But before she could elaborate any further, the door opened and in came the girls, already moaning about how hungry they were and how "old school" library systems were. Jill smiled as she began to prep the roast chicken her mother had bought that morning – only a few hours ago, though it felt like a lifetime. It really had been a long day, and bedtime couldn't come quickly enough for her.

To give her daughter some credit, Jill was grateful that Suzie at least waited until dinner was on the table before she started quizzing her grandmother about Martha King. Both Suzie and Melissa were practically bubbling over with details and nuggets of information that they had found in the library, from conspiracy theories to ghost stories and even a crystal ball gazer who claimed to be in contact with Martha from beyond the grave (that one creeped all of them out and the girls were quick to scoot over that particular example).

By the time they had finished, Rose was looking slightly shellshocked, though she composed herself quickly. Jill had always admired that in her mother; her ability to fix a smile and show the world the Rose they knew. As she continued the washing up, she gazed out of the window and noticed a magpie sitting on the fence post at the far end of the garden, looking almost directly at her. It was slightly disconcerting, and after a few seconds she turned away;

her thoughts returning to the room and the discussion that was going on around her.

'I'm afraid, love, there's not much more I know than that. The Martha King I knew wasn't some detective or mystical witch or ghost hunter – she was my grandmother, and she told the very best stories. Of course,' she said, glancing at Jill, 'some of them may have been a little more than just stories.'

Jill could tell that Suzie wanted more, but after a full day of research, her mind was competing between digging even deeper and succumbing to sleep. When Melissa finally suggested the two of them make their way upstairs to get ready for bed, Jill could have hugged her. The girls were still planning to visit London the following day, and Jill knew that if they didn't get to bed soon, they'd never be well-rested enough to enjoy the day completely. And if they deserved anything at all, it was a day to themselves in the city.

☉☉☉

As she climbed into bed that night, Jill found herself reaching for her own phone and tentatively typing "Martha King, Fulham Police" into the search engine. She didn't know what she would find – didn't even know what it was she hoped to find – but something was drawing her into this.

Twenty minutes later, she found what she was looking for.

At the bottom of a website posting old and historical newspaper clippings from a local village in Essex, there was an article listing the death of fourteen-year-old Henry Stone – a local boy who lived in one of the large houses that still stood proudly on the outskirts of Epping. The case had originally been ruled as an accidental death, but with the help of "local aid Martha King", two boys from a rival gang had been found guilty of manslaughter. The article went on to say that the evidence provided by Mrs King was thorough enough to formally charge the boys and that their confession came soon after. The boys had fallen into some sort of altercation at the side of the reservoir, and two boys had held Henry under the water as a threat. The tale didn't end well.

This article didn't have a photograph of Martha, but Jill didn't need one. The article referred to Martha as a "local aid" – the capacity of which was unclear and yet suddenly blindingly obvious to Jill. Maybe it was because she was so tired and overwhelmed, but as she sat in bed taking it all in, it hit her that what Martha had was a gift.

Call it magic, call it witchcraft, or call it unexplained and, quite frankly, terrifying. It was a gift, and by the looks of the articles they were slowly unearthing, Martha had been able to do some good, bringing justice to cases where crimes were unclear.

$$12$$

After saying goodnight to the others and closing her bedroom door, Rose hadn't gone to bed. Deep in the back of her wardrobe, there was a box that no one, not even Jill, had seen before. The box, a battered early edition Clarks shoe box if she wasn't mistaken, contained a set of letters and diaries that had been passed down through the generations of her family; small pieces of history that were theirs – well, hers now – and offered the one real look into the lives of those she was related to.

She loved these things and had always seen them as really priceless treasures. But now, of course, they were more than that. There was a diary that had belonged to Martha – one Rose had never before felt inclined to read, and yet now knew she had no choice. She shook her head as she relived Suzie's tale from that morning, and the gut-wrenching feeling that had spread across her body as she realised her own granddaughter sounded exactly like her grandmother had all those years ago.

Like some of Martha's stories, Suzie's story too had been a tale of trauma. It had to mean something.

The tales began in January 1909, and as Rose read them, she sensed a definite change in tone – from terror and confusion to trepidation and, eventually, a definite ease and confidence. Some of the stories dealt with crimes and murders, and Rose found a couple of them difficult to stomach – even just through the words scrawled on the page. Other stories were lighter, sharing anecdotes of women who wanted to know the sex of their unborn baby. One particular incident stood out to Rose, and as she read Martha's words, she almost laughed out loud at the obvious disdain with which her grandmother had shared this particular story.

It seemed as though a male colleague at the station hadn't believed Martha could tell the sex of an unborn baby of one of the office girls and had said so in front of quite a crowd. Rose remembered her grandmother as a headstrong woman and could almost picture Martha standing up as she set about proving herself to a room full of men.

⊙⊙⊙

Well, I tell you now, I wasn't having any of that, so I told him I could do better than just the sex of the baby. I could tell him exactly when and where the baby would be born – and the name.

Well, obviously he laughed, and all his buddies joined in. Elizabeth was five months pregnant at that stage, and as they all went back to their silly desk jobs, I bet they didn't think any of us would remember this in a few months' time.

But look who's laughing now! Born today, Tuesday 5th September, a little girl named Abigail.

Exactly what I told them and wrote down in the sealed envelope almost four months ago.

⊙◉◎

As Rose came to the end of the story, she once again recalled her grandmother's cheeky, infectious laugh and sense of humour. She could almost hear her reading the stories aloud to a young Rose who hung on every word.

Of course, by that time, Martha was much older – married to Rose's Grandad Joe and fully settled down. The diary's last entry was made at the end of 1915, when a quick entry revealed the date of their wedding and that they were now expecting their first child.

Rose supposed that Martha's undercover work must have slowed and eventually stopped as she transitioned into domestic life and spending time as a mother, but she could definitely sense pride in the tone of Martha's writing, which implied she had enjoyed the work she did with the police. Not only that, but she had clearly enjoyed winding her colleagues up too – with a handful of other tales similar to the baby reveal.

Rose eventually put the diary down and settled herself into her bed, sleep finally overcoming her.

13

Meanwhile, across the hall, Melissa and Suzie were getting themselves ready for bed. They had spent the past hour tracing maps of London, choosing a route for their day tomorrow and working out where they would be able to find the best bargains London had to offer.

As she was climbing into bed, Melissa was taken aback to see Suzie wearing the charity shop pyjamas from the previous night; the white material appeared almost ghostly in their phones' dim light.

'Are you really wearing them again?' she asked her friend cautiously. Suzie had been quiet all evening, and the last thing Melissa wanted to do was upset her even more, but she couldn't help feeling that the pyjamas were a bad omen.

Immediately, Suzie brushed her off as she lay down in bed. 'You've read too many ghost stories today, Mel,' she said, yawning. 'They're just pyjamas.'

☉☉☉

It was 3.07am when Melissa first stirred, abruptly coming to as she looked around for what had woken her. Suzie was writhing around on her bed, muttering in a panicked undertone that Melissa couldn't understand but which was clearly causing her friend a lot of grief.

Trying to remember everything she had read about waking sleeping people and how best to bring them around without furthering their panic, Melissa gently held Suzie's shoulders and very gently shook her until the muttering ceased and Suzie opened her eyes. Grabbing the glass of water from beside her bed, Melissa watched her friend, concerned and uneasy about what she had just witnessed. This was her oldest friend, and they had enjoyed countless sleepovers over the years – never before had Suzie behaved like this though.

'How long was I dreaming for?' asked Suzie groggily, rubbing her eyes as she looked over at the clock and then flopped back down on her pillow. 'I feel really rough.'

'I think you were dreaming again… was it the same as last night?'

Suzie nodded slowly. 'It felt longer this time though, you know, my dream… it was exactly like before, the walk and the drive and then getting home and everything everyone was saying was the same, but instead of me waking up at the same point as last time, I dreamt a bit more.'

'What happened?'

As they talked, Suzie retelling the same story that had first shocked them all less than twenty-four hours earlier, Melissa found herself shivering. She knew they had to tell Jill and Rose.

Creeping down the hallway towards Jill's bedroom door, Melissa used the wall to steady herself as she tiptoed past Rose's door, not wanting to wake the older woman. There was a large painting in the wide hallway that depicted a stream and a farmhouse-style cottage, and – not for the first time – she found her eyes drawn to the wildlife in the background, finding comfort in the birds that rested on tree branches and the sheep grazing in a field in the fore-ground of the painting. Turning away, she quietly knocked on the door.

Jill, unable to sleep much herself, was already awake, and when she saw Melissa's pale and worried face peering around her door, she jumped out of bed. She collected her dressing gown from the back of the door and continued behind Melissa until they reached their bedroom.

As Suzie told her what she had seen this time around, Jill stroked her hair and listened carefully, trying to align what they had learnt the previous day with what her daughter was telling her now. The stories they had unearthed about Martha certainly matched Suzie's in terms of the vivid dreams and realistic attention to detail, but what concerned Jill were the actions that Suzie was seeing and experiencing in her dreams. Martha may have played witness to goings on, but it seemed as though Suzie was herself experiencing what she saw – could the story she was telling really be playing out somewhere?

Jill dreaded to think of anyone being dragged up the stairs towards an unknown fate and found herself inclined to knock this on the head before it could go any further. She had a feeling that nothing good could come out of this – but she kept her mouth shut and listened as Suzie finished her story and fell quiet.

Glancing at the clock, Jill could see it was nearing 5am by now, and the sun was beginning to peep in around the curtains – a new day had dawned.

'Let's wait until your grandma's up, then we can decide what to do. In the meantime, I'll go make us all some coffee.'

Jill went downstairs to make the coffee, and as she was standing over the sink filling the kettle, she once again looked out towards the garden, considering what she had just heard.

Suzie's story had gone further this time. She had reached the bedroom, where she had found herself thrown onto the floor by the unknown man, only this time it hadn't stopped there. Whether it was a vision or a horribly vivid dream or something else – Suzie had then found herself taken back downstairs, again by the hair, screaming and crying for relief – but it never came. She couldn't recount all the details, it had been too horrible for that – but Suzie had told them the man was shouting a lot, indecipherable words, and threats and that she had tried to run away.

That was when she woke up.

Jill's gaze landed on a magpie – was it the same magpie she had seen yesterday? Just for a moment she found herself lost in a world of mystery and unknown. She had never been one to believe in ghost stories or spirits, but after spending the day reading about Martha's unexplained visions and hearing Suzie's recounting such awful but realistically vivid dreams, she started to wonder what it all meant.

For a second, staring at the magpie, she almost wondered if it was trying to tell her something. But then almost as swiftly as it had appeared, the magpie was gone.

☉☉☉

By the time Jill got back upstairs, Rose was up and sat on the end of Suzie's bed. As Jill threw open the curtains to let some light in, she spotted the magpie once again, sitting on one of the wires just metres from the window.

'This is the second night in a row now, love,' Rose was saying soothingly.

'But it's like each time I dream, I'm unfolding a little bit more of a story… only I have no control over it,' said Suzie, her head resting lightly against the headboard as she turned her face towards her mother.

'Like, the first night I had the dream, I was in my own house with my so-called mum's "partner", and he was really arguing and getting quite violent. Then last night, although I dreamt that again, it went on a bit more... I was in my bedroom in that house getting my phone.'

'I got to that point and then it all changed. Suddenly the guy was pulling me to the stairs and dragging me downstairs into the kitchen... I can't tell it again.' She looked pleadingly at her mum, who nodded and gave Rose a look that said, "I'll tell you later."

Jill went to put her arms round her daughter and gave her a big hug, just like she used to when her daughter needed her when she was young.

Right now, this was one of those moments when her daughter needed her. At this point, Suzie got quite emotional and upset; tears were falling down her face.

Jill felt helpless, her daughter was so upset, but there wasn't a thing she could do about it. Suzie looked so fragile.

'Are you still going into London today, you two girls?' asked Jill, looking towards Melissa for some backup.

'I... think so. Suze?'

'Yes, sure, I'm still up for it if you are,' Suzie replied, immediately lifting her chin a little and pulling away from her mother.

Jill had never felt so proud of her. 'That's what I was hoping you were going to say. I think it will do you the world of good,' she said, smiling at Melissa. 'You can do some shopping, go for something to eat and forget about everything for a few hours.'

As Jill got up to leave the girls so they could get ready, Rose went over to be with her granddaughter. Rose sat down next to her and gave her a hug.

'I know I said everything I could yesterday, but I'll rack my brains today, really, I will. See if I can remember anything else Martha might have told me.'

Suzie didn't need to say anything; she just nodded. As she turned away, Rose's face fell – the warm smile she had worn for her granddaughter dissolved into something else. Whatever this was, it scared her. She may not remember much about Martha, but whatever it was that possessed or influenced her, it hadn't always been easy for her. And goodness knows, she didn't want that same stress and anxiety taking hold of her only granddaughter.

14

The girls took turns getting themselves showered and dressed. Suzie felt relaxed in the shower – more relaxed than she had for the past couple of days – the warmth of the water raining down on her momentarily leaving her feeling warm and comforted.

By the time they got downstairs for breakfast, Jill and Rose were finishing up, muttering in hushed tones over the sink. As soon as the girls walked in, Jill immediately stopped talking and turned the radio up, offering the girls coffee and toast.

'You've got a busy day ahead of you!'

As the old classic "Walking on sunshine" by Katrina and The Waves came on the radio, Jill was relieved to see some of the tension start to leave her daughter's eyes as she and her friend chatted about where they wanted to go in London and the things they wanted to buy. The sun was shining, and the birds were singing – but more importantly, the trauma of the night before seemed to have passed. For now.

⊙◉◎

After the girls had waved goodbye to her at the tube station, Jill took a few moments to herself in the car. Today she planned to stay at home and do some gardening – the weather was too sunny for them to ignore the garden, and she knew her mum wanted to plant a new rose bush and tidy up some of the hedges. Up until now the week hadn't exactly been going to plan, and Jill was relieved that the girls were occupying their time with something other than exploring the sordid story of Suzie's dream and the history of her great-grandmother's police involvement.

⊙◉◎

As she pulled into the drive at home, Suzie and Melissa were just arriving in London. Jumping off the tube at Oxford Street, the girls made their way towards street level, planning on getting a bit of browsing out the way before enjoying a leisurely lunch somewhere outside.

They were all too aware that this was their last summer together before university, and while they were excited to get going and find some great outfits for the Freshers nights out, it was important to them to spend time together.

The air was light and warm, but as the two of them rounded the corner towards the South side of Oxford Street, Melissa felt a sudden sharp tug on her bag strap. Clutching the bag to her chest, she spun around, expecting to come face to face with a bag snatcher, but instead found herself looking straight into Suzie's – now pale – face.

'What's up?' asked Melissa, pulling Suzie to one side, out of the way of the hordes of shoppers.

Suzie didn't reply; she just allowed herself to be pulled back towards the shops, looking like she'd seen a ghost.

'What is it, Suzie?' pushed Melissa.

'I need to get away from here quickly.'

'I don't understand, Suzie. What's happening?' Melissa looked wildly around her, wondering if Suzie had seen a burglar or an accident on the road. Oxford Street was notorious for pedestrians acting stupidly, and it wouldn't be a surprise to see someone stepping out onto the road without checking the traffic first.

'I can't... not yet... but just take a good look at that guy behind the newspaper stand. Over there, on the corner by the steps. Then carry on walking. I'll explain in a minute.' She indicated with a quick nod over her shoulder.

Melissa, utterly confused, looked over Suzie's shoulder at the guy at the newspaper stand. He looked ordinary enough; middle-aged, with brown hair, a bit dirty and butch looking, she supposed, but nothing outstandingly different. He was holding a paper out towards a city worker, who looked like he was in a rush – briefcase hanging by his side, his hand pushing through his slightly tousled hair. The newsstand guy held out the paper and accepted the change. As she stared, the man looked up, directly at her for just a few seconds before his gaze moved on to the next customer. Just an average guy.

The girls hurried down Oxford Street, past Next and New Look, not even glancing into the shop windows at the pastel shades and polka dot patterns that define their summer wardrobes. Past Marks & Spencer and Primark. Turning left, they made their way past a fancy hotel and a Nando's, arriving at a small café that sat two roads back from Oxford Street itself.

Suzie finally slowed, opened the door, and led them to a small table towards the centre of the café.

As they sat down, one of the waitresses came up to them, smiling and asking for their order. In unison, the girls both asked for a skinny hazelnut iced latte, smiling for a minute at their similar tastes.

But it wasn't long before Suzie's face fell back into the grimace she had been wearing since they got off the tube.

'What's wrong, Suzie?' asked Melissa.

'That guy at the newspaper stand, you saw him, right?'

Melissa nodded slowly, unsure if she was meant to have recognised him.

'That guy... well, he looked like... no, he WAS, the guy I've been seeing in my dreams for the past two nights. The same guy, Melissa.'

Gobsmacked, Melissa struggled for words. 'But, how do you know? I mean, are you SURE?'

Suzie glared at her. 'I'm not making it up, Melissa. If you don't believe me, then fine, but...'

'No, no, it's not that. Why wouldn't I believe you? It's just... are you sure it's not somebody who just looks like him?' Catching sight of Suzie's face, Melissa hastily added, 'Let's go back there. I'm with you, so there's no need to be afraid. That way we can get a better look at him... see if he really is the guy in your dream.'

At that moment, they were interrupted by the waitress bringing over their coffees, giving Suzie chance to reflect on what she had seen and Melissa some time to mull it over in her head. Whatever she had been expecting from this trip down South with Suzie's family, it certainly wasn't a week like this.

A good hour later, they were stepping back onto Oxford Street and wandering up against the flow of the crowds, using their hands to shield their eyes from the late morning sun.

As they approached the newspaper stand, Melissa stepped forward boldly and started flicking through the magazines. After a moment's hesitation, Suzie joined her.

'You gonna buy that love, or do you just like the way it feels in your hand?'

The voice made both of them jump, Suzie only just concealing a squeal that threatened to escape her lips. Melissa answered with a forced laugh.

'Sorry, yes. Um... how much?'

As she fumbled around for some change, Suzie couldn't tear her eyes away from the man. His toothy grin made her want to shudder, while his greying polo shirt and hat added years to the face that she had originally assumed to be much older than he was. Closer up, the guy looked to be in his early forties.

As she stared, his voice cut through her like a knife. 'You alright there, love?'

She looked away quickly.

Having finally located enough change for the magazine, Melissa handed the guy his money. As he took it, Suzie noticed that each of his fingers was decorated with a small star tattoo.

Almost as if reading her friend's mind, Melissa piped up, 'What are those tattoos for? Do they mean anything?'

Almost as soon as the words had left her mouth, she wished she hadn't asked. The guy frowned slightly before smiling widely again.

'You're a nosey one, aren't you? Nah, they don't mean anything in particular, just a very permanent memory from a very drunken night out.'

With that, he turned away and started serving the next customer who had wandered over in search of chewing gum.

As they walked away, Melissa nudged Suzie on the arm. 'Hey, you've got something on him now. If you dream about it again and you see him, look for those tattoos. If he's got them, you know he's your guy.'

'Yes, and what if he does?' asked Suzie. 'What exactly does that mean? It means I've seen him before, and that he could be a very dangerous person.'

15

As the day wore on, Oxford Street got steadily busier, and Suzie found herself more irritated than normal as other shoppers barged into her and whipped her with their shopping bags. After an hour or so of fruitless browsing and trying things on, Melissa suggested they make a lunch stop. So, they found the nearest Italian and sat outside, ordered pasta and a glass of wine.

After a light lunch and a great deal of people-watching, the girls decided that the afternoon would be best spent lazing around Hyde Park, enjoying the sunshine and chatting about their plans for university and beyond.

Walking past a Mayfair bakery on their way, they let their senses take over as they followed the lovely smells and bought some pastries for their breakfast the next day.

Hyde Park was heaving with families gathered around the ice cream truck, throwing balls back and forth and messing around on the boating lake. Couples lay on their backs sunbathing while groups of friends gathered in the shade of the large trees, sipping from cans, and playing music through their portable speakers. The atmosphere just screamed of a lazy summer day, and Suzie felt herself relaxing for the first time since they had arrived in London; such was the pleasantness of the day.

◉◉◉

After a couple of hours, when the family groups started to pack up, and the groups of friends meandered off – probably in search of more beer or more of a party vibe – the girls decided to call it a day.

It was only as they approached Oxford Street station that Suzie remembered the newspaper guy – sure enough, there he was, counting change and stacking papers in a trolley next to his stand. He looked up as they passed and gave Suzie a slight nod, causing her insides to shrivel up momentarily.

'I don't like him,' hissed Suzie, nodding towards him as Melissa followed her gaze.

'There's definitely something a bit off about him,' agreed Melissa. But before she could say anything else, the two of them were swept along in a rush of commuters and tourists onto the tube train and back towards Epping.

◉◉◉

Later that evening, after finishing the washing up from dinner, Suzie told her mum and grandma about the guy they'd seen in London. They didn't know what to say. Jill was adamant she would go back with Suzie tomorrow to see the guy again and try to make sense of it all, but Suzie wasn't having any of it.

'What exactly are you going to say, Mum? My daughter saw you in a nightmare, and now she thinks you're some psychopath. No way.' She shook her head and stood to leave, Melissa close behind.

It was still warm and light outside, so Suzie and Melissa decided to go sit outside and enjoy the sunset. Armed with glasses of iced coke, a couple of magazines and their favourite playlist, they settled themselves in the deck chairs at the back of the house.

While the girls soaked up the last of the summer day, Jill headed upstairs to get herself ready for bed, passing the girls' shopping bags on the way. Jill knew her daughter well and was surprised to see just one item in the bag she had seen Suzie carrying – a pair of short silky pyjamas. Not unusual per se, but a little odd given that Suzie had similar pairs back home in Leeds but had preferred her old T-shirts and shorts.

Jill wondered if Suzie was trying not to hurt her grandma's feelings by pretending she liked the charity shop pyjamas, or if it was something more. Perhaps Suzie felt uncomfortable wearing them after the trauma of the last couple of nights.

She made a note to ask Suzie about it in the privacy of their bedroom later, away from Rose's sharp ears. Goodness knows her mother felt bad enough about all the nightmares going around and the links to her relatives – she didn't need to add a bad charity shop purchase to her list.

The girls made their way inside after an hour or so in the garden and headed upstairs to their bedroom. After they'd had chance to get themselves ready for bed, Jill took the girls a hot chocolate up and perched on Suzie's bed. Suzie was sitting upright on her bed, legs crossed, and Melissa was lying on her stomach, reading her magazine.

'Did you girls get anything nice today?' The two of them shrugged, Melissa got up from the bed and showed Jill a jumper she'd purchased in a sale. Suzie said nothing, but Jill pushed on. 'Not wearing your grandma's pyjamas, Suze?' she asked.

Suzie shook her head. 'Not tonight. I think it's a little warm for them actually.'

Jill knew it was time to go to bed and give it a rest, but she couldn't resist one last question. 'You don't think... you don't reckon the pyjamas have got anything to do with your dreams, do you? You're not worried...?' Before she could finish her sentence, Suzie was shaking her head adamantly.

'No,' she said quickly, her laugh a little stilted. 'Grandma washed them before giving them to me, and the charity shop told Grandma that they were as good as new.'

Jill nodded. 'Ok, love, goodnight both of you,' she said, backing out of the room.

After the girls had finished their hot chocolate and listened to the end of their playlist, they decided it was time to call it a day. Once again, a lot had happened, and both were looking forward to getting some sleep.

⊚⊚⊚

A few hours later, Melissa woke up to go to the bathroom. As she got out of bed, she looked over at her friend, almost afraid of what sight would greet her. The last two nights had been difficult for her, seeing her friend in such distress, and she wasn't sure how much more she could take. Her eyes landed on Suzie's sleeping silhouette; Melissa was relieved to see that Suzie looked quite peaceful. For now, it seemed, she wasn't having any nightmares.

Melissa went to the bathroom and returned to her bed – not waking up again until late the next morning.

16

Hearing her mother stirring in the next room, Suzie glanced at the clock. 8.30am. She wasn't sure how long she had been awake; what she did know, however, was that last night had been her first dreamless sleep since arriving in Epping.

The previous two nights, ridden with trauma and fear, were starting to become a blur, and try as she might, there were already details and images she was starting to forget.

She looked over at Melissa, but seeing she was still asleep, decided to leave her in peace for a bit. She deserved a lie-in after the drama that Suzie had brought to the last couple of mornings.

Slipping quietly out of bed, Suzie headed over to the window and, gathering a pillow to her chest, sat on the windowsill and gazed out at the garden. Gardens and outdoor spaces had always calmed her; ever since she was a child, she had always enjoyed watching the wildlife come and go – from birds to bugs, rabbits and other small mammals. Once, way back before her grandad had died, they had spotted an otter on one of the nearby nature reserves, creeping along the banks of the river behind reeds. Spellbound at the time, Suzie had never forgotten that otter, so independent and fearless.

Eventually, Melissa stirred, and after one last look out to the garden, Suzie turned to her friend.

'Hey, sleepyhead,' said Suzie.

'Now THAT was a good sleep,' Melissa exclaimed, stretching and picking up her phone to see the time. Seeing it had gone 9am, she was momentarily shocked at how late it was, then looked questioningly at Suzie. Suzie knew what she was asking and just shook her head in response.

'Nothing new, I slept straight through,' she confirmed.

'Must be those lovely new pyjamas you've been wearing then,' said Melissa with a grin, pulling herself out of bed and reaching for her dressing gown – before deciding it was already too hot for extra layers.

'Yeah, right.'

'Seriously,' said Melissa. 'You never know, do you? Could be those pyjamas are the answer to everything. The mystery of the magic pyjamas! The horrors of the heart-covered sleepwear.'

'The curse of the patterned flannel,' laughed Suzie, joining in. 'I don't care what you say,' she continued. 'I like them. And I'll wear them again tonight to prove it.'

17

As the group settled down for breakfast, talk inevitably turned to the day ahead – and the night before.

'What you girls up to today then?' asked Jill, cocking her head at her daughter. Suzie hadn't made any reference to how she had slept, and Jill was bursting to ask if the dreams had returned or not.

'Not sure, Mum, we haven't really thought about it yet!' replied Suzie, tucking into pastries the girls had bought the day before – giving nothing away.

'You seem in a really good, relaxed mood this morning, love,' said Jill, probing for more information.

'I feel great, Mum, honestly,' Suzie said, looking up with a smile. 'I was just telling Melissa upstairs. I've had a full night's sleep, no interruptions, and no weird dreams.'

Jill was noticeably relieved – her whole body relaxing a little. 'That's good. Maybe it really was nothing.' She looked hopefully at Rose, who simply nodded – looking a little wary. Jill decided to ignore her. 'Let's just forget it all and enjoy the rest of our stay!'

'I was thinking, though...' began Melissa uncertainly. 'It seems odd that Suzie only had those dreams when she wore the charity shop pyjamas... I know it sounds crazy,' she added hastily, 'but are we sure there isn't something more going on?'

Suzie, who had never known her friend to be anything other than a complete cynic, looked at Melissa in surprise. She knew Melissa didn't feel comfortable with the idea of her wearing second-hand pyjamas, but she didn't think that she actually believed in all this magic stuff.

'I don't think it's connected, love, don't go looking for things that aren't there,' replied Jill, a little more firmly than necessary.

Shrugging, Melissa stood, and the girls mooched upstairs, loosely discussing how they might spend the day. It didn't take long for them to land upon the perfect summer holiday plan – to just chill out and do nothing.

◉◉◉

After a day of rest and recuperation, the girls decided to stick with their plan and go out – only neither of them much fancied facing London again.

Instead of going into the city, the girls decided to keep it local and maybe head to the cinema, noting that there was a new horror film out that would not only keep them distracted, but would certainly give them something to talk to the boys about when they got home. Simon and Max would hardly believe that they had paid to see a horror film!

After a couple of cocktails in Epping's finest bar – The Speakeasy – they opted for the 9pm showing of a horror called "The Children"; a film where the children gradually became increasingly psychotic with the influence of a terrifying nanny, to the point that they killed their own parents.

In hindsight, perhaps not the best choice given her recent nightmares, Suzie thought as they left the cinema and headed home. By the time they reached the front door, the lights were out; both Rose and Jill were already in bed, sound asleep and finally free from worry. For now.

18

When they got to their room, the girls were touched to see their beds freshly made, a glass of water beside each of them, and their pyjamas folded neatly at the end of the beds. Picking up her new silk short set, Suzie considered them for a moment before putting them down and reaching for the flannel charity shop pair.

'You're not really going to wear them, are you?' asked Melissa, glancing over as she got dressed. Suzie nodded defiantly. 'Suzie, you don't have to. You've made your point.'

But Suzie pulled the pyjamas on and got into bed without another word. For some reason she felt a weird nervous sensation, like she was entering dangerous territory. Ridiculous, she thought. You're being ridiculous. They're just pyjamas.

After a few minutes of chatter, the girls eventually drifted off – Melissa watching her friend cautiously as her eyes began to flutter with sleep. Suzie was wearing the pyjamas to prove a point – not just to Melissa but to herself as well. Melissa knew her well enough to know that when Suzie got an idea in her head, you couldn't talk her out of it, but she wished her friend would just let this dream stuff go. It was like Suzie felt some pull of responsibility towards the dream – like it was something only she could solve, which was crazy! Wasn't it?

⊙◉⊚

'Come on, love,' Jill said, shaking Suzie gently while Melissa watched on anxiously. 'Wake up, come on.'

Suzie's eyes suddenly opened, and she sat bolt upright, causing Jill and Melissa to step back in a mixture of surprise and horror.

'Where am I?' said Suzie groggily, as her body suddenly sagged and she slumped against the headboard.

'It's okay, love, you're in Gran's spare bedroom with Melissa.'

'You were shaking and crying, and I didn't know what to do, Suze. I'm sorry,' said Melissa, almost tearful now. Suzie just shook her head and smiled weakly at her friend, but the smile didn't reach her eyes. There, she didn't give anything away; her eyes were blank.

'She died, Mum, I saw it. Last time I woke up just as he came at her – or at me, I don't know which – but this time I couldn't wake up. I wanted to, but I couldn't and suddenly I knew that was it. That was the end. But I couldn't wake up.' She started to cry as she said the words, but when Jill went to put her arm around her, Suzie shook her head animatedly.

'No, I have to say this. He took the body – my body – and wrapped it in a rug. It was me, but then suddenly it wasn't me, and I was just watching as he put her – me – in a rug and carried her outside.'

She paused, and the room was deadly silent. Jill and Melissa didn't even know what to say.

'That's when I woke up,' ended Suzie.

Jill looked at the clock – 3.35am. They were all tired; Melissa had woken Jill up when she couldn't get Suzie to calm down. She was glad she had; she didn't want her daughter to face this – whatever it was – alone, and she was glad Melissa was there too.

'Come on, love, let's get you settled down,' Jill said, putting her arm around her daughter. This time, Suzie let her. 'This is getting too much for you now. It can wait until morning.'

As an afterthought, she added, 'Why don't you put something else on to wear? I'm not saying it is the pyjamas but, well, you might sleep better without these on, eh? Maybe you're just too hot!' she threw in, taking inspiration from the sweat she could see running down Suzie's forehead. That must be it, the pyjamas were simply too thick for the summer nights, and the heat was making Suzie suffer from these awful dreams.

Suzie, too tired and emotionally drained to argue, agreed to change and allowed her mum to pass the short silky pyjamas she'd worn the night before. 'I just need to sleep; I feel completely worn out and I think I've got a heavy headache coming on as well.'

As Jill helped settle her daughter back down, Melissa watched on quietly. She was glad Suzie was okay and couldn't help but feel a little jealous of how much Jill cared about her. Suzie was lucky to have a mum like Jill, so loving and invested in her daughter's life. Miles apart from her own mum. As she felt her eyes start to drift shut, she saw Jill stand, blow her a kiss and a little wave, and head back to her own room.

Whatever it was, they'd deal with it in the morning.

19

It was nearly 10am when the girls finally surfaced and decided it was time to get up.

'How you feeling?' Melissa asked Suzie as they trudged downstairs, a little blurry-eyed in the bright sunshine.

'Not bad. I didn't have that dream again if that's what you're wondering.'

As they entered the kitchen, Jill was already bustling around making breakfast; Rose watched on, holding a mug of steaming coffee. As soon as she saw the girls, Rose stood up and threw her arms around Suzie. Jill had obviously told her what had happened, Melissa thought, as she watched the show of affection.

As Jill carried on cracking eggs into a pan, Rose shooed the girls back upstairs, telling them today was a day for breakfast in bed.

Fifteen minutes later, Jill made her way upstairs with the girls' breakfasts on a tray. Jill put the tray down on the bedside cabinet and sat down on Suzie's bed.

'Right, Suzie,' said Jill, in a matter-of-fact tone that caught the girls a little off guard. Jill continued, 'I know you don't want to hear this, but your grandma and I were talking yesterday. Now, I'm not one for believing in spooky stuff, and I'm as lost as you are when it comes to these dreams. HOWEVER, over the last few nights, I've seen for myself what disturbing things can take place, and I don't like what I'm seeing, particularly when it involves my own daughter. Your grandma and I have discussed the old Martha stories and looked at her diaries, and we think we've found a pattern. Objects, things she touched, items she came into contact with. Well, we want to try something out... and hear me out before you say anything...

'We really do think that those pyjamas...' she gestured towards the pyjamas that were lying discarded on a chair, '... you're wearing, the ones your grandma got from the charity shop the other week, have something to do with it.' She held up a hand to silence the protests that Suzie looked set to throw at her.

'Your grandma washed everything, but it still seems as though the girl's spirit is... tied to them somehow.' She waved a hand around, and both girls could tell that she wasn't feeling entirely comfortable with what she was saying. But whether she believed it or not, they all knew it was something they had to consider.

After all, Martha had first seen what she saw when she touched that jacket. The diary said so.

After a pause, Jill continued. 'Now I've been thinking. If – and it's a massive if – but IF you are in some way linked to Martha, then we have to look at why she continued to see what she saw. She saw things in order to help – solving crimes, putting people to rest, contacting and passing on messages to family members – everything she saw had a purpose. And if we are to link this, what's happening to you, in some way, then it only makes sense to assume that you are seeing all this for a reason too.'

She held up a hand again, but this time there was no need. Suzie and Melissa were stunned into silence, each lost in their own thoughts, considering what Jill had said and allowing it to fit in place.

Suzie slowly nodded and looked at her mum. 'I think I'm seeing her die, Mum. What can I do? Should I be stopping it from happening, or... has it already happened?'

She looked desperately around, her eyes brimming with sudden tears.

'I think,' her mum said gently, 'that she needs your help to rest in peace. That something about this isn't right, that there's something the family doesn't know. Something that maybe you can help to uncover,' she finished, thinking back to the article she had read about the little boy who had drowned, and the truth that Martha had helped to uncover for his family.

'You've got to find her, Suzie, and get that man locked up,' came a voice from the doorway. Rose was there, framed by the light from the landing window. The others hadn't heard her approaching, but looking at her now, Suzie could see a proud smile on her face. 'It's what Martha would have done, love, and you're just like her. You care, Suzie, and you can use this to help that girl and her family.'

Jill squeezed Suzie's hand as Suzie wiped her eyes and nodded at her grandma. Rose held up Martha's most recent diary.

'Martha was scared at first when she saw stuff. You can tell just from the way she writes. At first, the visions she sees are so short because she drops the object as soon as she sees anything.'

She flicks through the pages until she lands on the one she is looking for.

'Here, she says, "*As I picked up the jacket, suddenly I wasn't in the storeroom anymore. I was on the street outside; one I didn't recognise. I was so shocked, I dropped the jacket, and suddenly I was back – like a bad dream gone wrong.*" As soon as she stopped touching the object, the vision stopped. It takes a long time,' Rose flicked through the later pages as she spoke, 'but over time, as she got used to what was happening, she managed to hold on for longer and let the scene play out.'

She looked up at her granddaughter and could see from the look in Suzie's eye that she, too, knew what she had to do.

'You've got to let me sleep through,' Suzie said slowly as the others looked on – Jill concerned, Rose adamant, and Melissa trying her best to hold it together.

Jill was the first to speak, turning to Melissa. 'Okay, but Melissa, I still want you to wake me up because I will sit with Suzie while she's dreaming.'

'I need to be woken up, too,' added Rose. 'I don't want my granddaughter mixed up in this without me beside her.'

Suddenly the responsibility and fear began to overwhelm Suzie. 'Hang on here, you all automatically think I'm going to dream this really horrible dream again, but what if I don't? I can't make myself dream it, you know. I don't get to choose,' she cried.

'That's it, and if you can't, that's okay. But if you do dream that terrible dream again, we will be here for you,' Jill said, grabbing her daughter's hand. 'Of course, if you don't and you're still wearing the pyjamas, then it can't be them,' she said adamantly, looking now towards her mother.

'Let's face facts, Suzie, you've worn them three times now, and you've had the same nightmare all three times. That's not just a coincidence,' chipped in Rose.

'We don't even know where the pyjamas came from or who owned them before,' carried on Suzie. She didn't know who she was trying to convince, but a small part of her didn't want to accept the fate she knew she had to face. 'I mean, who's to say they don't belong to someone your age, Mum, or yours Grandma!' she added.

Jill shook her head. 'They definitely belong to somebody your age. That's why your grandma bought them for you, love.'

Suzie sighed. The battle was over.

'Okay. I'll wear them. In fact, I'm feeling pretty tired today, to be honest.' She reached for the pyjamas. 'If it's okay with Melissa,' she added, looking at her friend, 'I'll just stay in today and wear them all day. We'll see what happens. And if I do have the dream again, well then, I might just go to the charity shop myself and find out where they came from. They might remember if it was someone local.' She smiled at them, pleased with her new plan. Finally, she felt like she was taking back control.

As they all stood, Rose began to speak.

'The thing I can't get my head round is that I wasn't going to buy the pyjamas. I mean, it's a bit different from what you might expect to buy, particularly second-hand. But the lady must have seen what I was buying and deliberately brought them to my attention. She said that the girl they belonged to had only worn them a handful of times. To be honest, they were so cheap that I didn't even think to ask why they had been sent to the charity shop and knew they'd only been worn a few times. Come to think of it, I didn't even ask how she knew this... I just thought that if Suzie didn't like them, she could give them to somebody else or I would take them back to the charity shop!'

Jill leant over and gave Suzie a kiss. 'Come on, love, you two have your breakfast, it's getting cold. Then come downstairs. It's beautiful out today. Why don't we potter about, and I'll help Grandma in the garden. There's no point wasting our last few days here, what with all this wonderful sunshine!'

As she finished speaking, she realised Suzie was barely listening; her eyes were fixed on the window. A magpie sat perched on the windowsill, its head cocked towards them, a steely look in its beady eye.

'That magpie,' Suzie said slowly, nodding at it. 'Every time I've dreamt about the girl, there's a magpie sat on that window ledge in the morning. And yesterday, when I hadn't dreamt about the girl and didn't wear the pyjamas, the magpie wasn't there...'

She shook her head. 'God, Mum, I'm as bad as the rest of you. I sound like a crazy person.' She laughed drily. 'Let's get up, shall we?'

'I don't think your crazy at all love and for the magpie, I've seen it a couple of times over the last few days as well. It was staring at me, like it's doing now.'

'Probably just a coincidence,' Melissa agreed as the girls hustled the adults out of the room so they could have their breakfast.

When they'd both finished, Suzie jumped out of bed and reached into the drawer for a T-shirt when she remembered her promise to put the pyjamas back on. Sighing, she reached for the flannel top and pulled it on, grimacing.

Jill was pleased that Suzie was suddenly so open, telling them everything. Suzie and Jill had always told each other everything. With it just the two of them for so long, they had a bond she treasured beyond everything else. She knew she was lucky that way – Melissa never confided in her mum, she had said so a number of times over the years, and if anything, to Jill it felt like she too had started to confide more in Jill as well as Suzie.

Having thought back over what had just been discussed, Jill knew a lot of people would think Suzie was mad. And yet, she knew that her daughter needed help. Suzie wouldn't lie about this. When she woke after one of her nightmares, the look in her eyes was enough to tell Jill that this was serious.

20

Melissa stood at the top of the stairs, waiting for Suzie to come out of the bathroom so the two of them could head downstairs together. As comfortable as she felt around Suzie's family, with all this uncertainty in the air, she didn't feel 100% comfortable around Rose and Jill without Suzie by her side. The way Jill looked at her, like she felt sorry for her, made Melissa feel a bit awkward.

No, much better to wait for Suzie and go down together.

But as she stepped out of the bathroom, Suzie's eyes were fixed on the wall ahead of her, passing over Melissa completely as she stepped onto the first step.

'Hey!' said Melissa before she could stop herself. 'Had you forgotten about me?' Suzie looked at her vacantly. 'Are you okay?' she added carefully.

Suzie shook her head, then nodded quickly. 'Yes, sure, why?'

'Well,' Melissa took a deep breath. 'For a start, I was waiting for you. You just ignored me. You saw me waiting for you to go down. Why didn't you wait?'

'Just didn't think, sorry,'

'It's just… it's not like you,' Melissa finished, hanging her head. She wasn't sure why she was being so precious. She was being ridiculous. What did it matter if Suzie waited for her or not?

The girls went down quietly. But Melissa knew things weren't right. As Suzie went into the living room and melted into the sofa, Melissa switched on the TV for her before heading for the kitchen. Time to get over herself and speak to Jill and Rose directly.

But as she saw Jill and Rose smiling, chatting lightly about what jobs they could do around the garden that day, she stopped short. Who was she to ruin their day with more of her fears and worries?

As she joined Suzie back in the living room, Melissa gestured towards the kitchen, where she could faintly hear the others discussing herb beds and seasonal planting.

'Hey, you wouldn't get me doing jobs in the garden on a hot day like this unless it's to sunbathe,' she laughed, a forced chuckle, then looked at Suzie. It was as if she hadn't heard a word.

'Did you hear me, Suzie? I said...'

'Yes, I heard you,' Suzie said quietly.

Melissa sat next to Suzie on the sofa and put her arms around her. She didn't know what else she could do. 'Suze, what's up? You can tell me, please...'

'What, oh nothing, Melissa, what's wrong? Did you say something?'

'No,' Melissa shook her head. 'Nothing in particular.' She stayed next to Suzie for a while, the two of them vaguely watching an old episode of Friends.

When Melissa went upstairs to get her new nail varnish she'd bought from their trip to London – she figured, if they were sitting inside all day, she might as well get something productive done – she left Suzie gazing absentmindedly at the television. When she returned, her friend was sound asleep.

'Crikey, that was quick,' Melissa muttered to herself, putting down the nail varnish and heading outside to let Jill and Rose know.

When she told them Suzie was asleep, the three of them just stood looking at each other for a moment, not quite knowing what to do next. They would have to just wait and see what happened.

Jill broke the silence. 'You do realise, don't you – and I know we're all thinking it – that Suzie is having flashbacks of the day that girl was killed? Am I right? It just sounds so farfetched,' she finished desperately.

Melissa looked at Jill. 'We could go to the police and do some digging with them? See if they have any recent reports about a young girl? If it has happened, I mean, if what Suzie is seeing has happened, they might have charged someone for her killing already. Suzie might not even have to do anything,' she added hopefully, already knowing that this was unlikely.

'I see where you're coming from, Melissa,' nodded Jill. 'I suppose what we're looking for, the answer we need, is in Suzie's dreams. It's like something's missing, the last piece of the jigsaw. We need to know how it ends, or we'll never get to the bottom of it.'

'Yes, well, we need to sort this out before you go back home, don't we?' said Rose decidedly. 'It's Thursday and you go home on Saturday. That's only two more nights to try and get Suzie through the dream, right to the end.'

'I was thinking about that. I think I have to stay on here longer with Suzie, but Melissa can go home as planned. It would be better to get this sorted while we're here instead of uprooting Suzie and forcing her to see this out in her own room, back home.' Jill nodded as she finished speaking, convincing herself that this definitely was the best plan for everyone.

'If it's okay with you,' piped up Melissa hopefully, 'well, okay with both of you and Suzie, of course, I would like to stay on as long as you are. I mean, I've got no plans back home, so...' she tailed off, looking from Rose to Jill.

Rose's face broke into a smile, the first smile Melissa had seen on her face in days.

'Of course you can stay, love. You can stay for as long as you like.' She put a hand on Melissa's arm and gave it a squeeze before turning back to Jill, who nodded.

'Right then, that's settled. We will stay as long as it takes to get Suzie better and make these nightmares stop,' said Jill. 'But as soon as you want to go home, Melissa, just say, and we will sort it out,' she added.

'Thanks, but if it's all the same to you, I will stay until we're all ready to go home. I want to be with Suzie, too, she's my best friend. My family,' Melissa finished. The three of them smiled at each other.

Decisions made, Rose and Jill turned their attention back to the garden as Melissa headed back inside to check on Suzie.

⊙⊙⊚

As Suzie was still asleep a couple of hours later, Jill and Rose decided to go to the Police Station and see if they could find anything out about a local girl who may be missing. Melissa had wracked her brain to give them the best description she could of the man they had seen on Oxford Street, the one Suzie had been so sure was the man in her dream, but as the other two walked out the front door she couldn't help but feel a bit useless.

Stuck in the house with only her sleeping friend for company, Melissa settled down on the sofa to watch television and picked up her nail varnish where she'd left it. She was in this for the long haul, and she had a feeling it wasn't going to be as straightforward as they were all pretending it could be.

21

'You know, I don't think the police are going to be able to tell us anything,' said Jill as she and her mother got out of the car and made their way up the steps of the local Epping Police Station.

'I mean, they're hardly going to just welcome us in and start sharing details of their investigations, are they? What exactly are we going to say to them? I mean, we don't know what this girl looks like. It might be something that happened years ago...'

Rose's mind started to tune out Jill's rambling worries, as she herself thought back to that morning in the charity shop the previous week. The lady had been so adamant that she take the pyjamas, even picking them off the shelf herself and handing them to Rose. They had been so cheap that she hadn't really thought twice.

'We've not *really* given this much thought at all, have we?' Jill's voice broke through Rose's thoughts as she stopped just short of the entrance.

'I was thinking,' she continued, 'the charity shop where you bought Suzie's clothes from was local, right? Which means the girl must be local!' She nodded at her own logic before continuing.

'Suzie saw the guy in her dreams in London, and London isn't so far away on the tube. So again, he must be pretty local too. Mum, we need to try and remember if there was anything on the news about a missing teenage girl in this area. There can't be many.'

'Shall we start at the library like the girls did the other day?' asked Rose, catching on to Jill's logic and desperately searching her memory for any stories she had seen on the news about a missing girl.

'Well, that's a better start, I suppose, than just coming here and hounding the local police,' commented Jill. 'Even better, why don't you go to the library with Melissa, as she knows what to do and I'll stay at home with Suzie and see what happens?'

The two of them turned and headed back to the car without going into the police station, confident in their new plan. Rose was glad she had a job to do and was intrigued by the opportunity to find out more about the visions her own ancestor had had.

'You could call in on the charity shop as well,' suggested Jill as an afterthought as they pulled back into the driveway. 'Maybe they'll remember who donated the pyjamas and be able to shed a little more light on where they came from.'

<h1 style="text-align:center">22</h1>

'You don't mind tagging along with me, do you, Melissa?' Rose asked as she got back into the car with the younger girl less than ten minutes later.

Melissa smiled at her and shook her head. 'You're joking, aren't you? This sure is better than sitting back at home in Leeds on my own every day! When Suzie's down here, I always feel a little lost up there on my own,' she admitted, not looking at Rose.

There was something about the old lady that she trusted, and that made her want to open up.

Rose nodded slowly. She knew little bits about Melissa's home life – not much, but enough to understand that the girl preferred to be with her friend than with her own family. 'You know you're always welcome, love, and you really are an amazing rock for our Suzie.'

'I feel a bit bad,' said Melissa after a moment. 'Here I am, glad to be able to stay here – happy, even – and then there's Suzie having the worst time of her life. She looks exhausted. It can't be any fun for her at all.'

'No love, you're probably right. But we can at least help her out and get to the bottom of this.'

Melissa decided to share an idea that had been forming in her head over the past couple of hours. 'You know, I've been thinking. The next time Suzie wakes up from a bad dream, she should write it down. That way it's something we can all go back to, to make sure every time is the same.'

'Brilliant idea, Melissa! Why don't you run back in and tell Jill in case Suzie wakes up while we're out?'

As Melissa jumped out of the car and made her way back up the path, Rose watched her go. Once this was over, she wasn't sure how the girls would ever go back to feeling normal – she realised, now, that Martha had never really led a normal life. Once she realised what her visions meant, it had changed her – not that Rose had known it then, but she could see it and hear it in the way Martha wrote her diary. Martha had spent the rest of her life bogged down by a pressure and sense of responsibility that she had never really been able to shake.

Rose just hoped the same thing didn't happen to Suzie and to Melissa – who was as much a part of this now as any of them.

☉☉☉

Back in the house, Suzie started to stir.

Jill, having just returned to the room with a pen and paper after waving Melissa and Rose off, stopped short and hesitated for a moment before taking a seat and watching her daughter closely – close enough to see her eyelashes twitching and hear the almost inaudible words that her daughter was whispering.

They made no sense, yet their urgency and panic were clear enough.

Ten more minutes passed, and Jill started to realise that Suzie's actions were becoming more and more aggressive. She didn't want to wake her – she knew how important it was that Suzie finish her dream by herself and wake herself up – but she didn't like to see her daughter like this. It was enough to cause any mother trauma.

The only thing that got her through it was the knowledge that another mother, somewhere else, probably didn't even know where her daughter was.

23

Pulling up a chair next to Rose, Melissa quickly logged onto the online newspaper archive list and started sifting through the editions – looking for anything with "missing teenager" in the subject line.

'It's a good job you're here with me, love,' said Rose, watching wide-eyed as Melissa's fingers flew across the keyboard. 'I would still be stuck knee-deep in newspapers off the shelves.' She chuckled – who knew that nowadays they scanned newspapers onto computers?

Melissa laughed and said, 'I only know because the lady showed us the other day. See here, you search for the area you want – let's stick with Epping for now – and then you can narrow the dates down. What do you think?'

Rose thought for a moment, then said, 'Let's start from January, from the beginning of the year. That's best, don't you think?'

Melissa stopped typing for a moment and looked up at Rose, her eyes dewy with unexpected emotion. 'What exactly am I looking for, Rose?' she asked, almost fearfully now.

'Keep it local. There must be something here, I do remember something from the local news about a girl who disappeared, but I can't remember if they found her. She could be our girl, I suppose…' Rose tailed off, and Melissa continued her search.

'I suppose when we've found who we are looking for, we can go to the charity shop with a picture of the girl and ask them if it was the girl's family who handed the pyjamas in,' Melissa announced with a newfound determination. 'That is, if the family actually handed the clothes into the charity shop themselves… sometimes people just leave bags of clothes on the doorstep.'

The two of them fell silent and didn't speak again until they reached the end of January.

No joy. No missing children or teenagers. The search continued.

It wasn't until the last week in February that they came across the story of Louise, an eighteen-year-old who looked so normal that, for a moment, Melissa couldn't breathe. Louise had long brown hair and big brown eyes – a kind face, like the kind of girl you would want to be friends with.

'That's her,' said Rose quietly. 'That's the girl that was on the news. I remember her hair. It reminded me of Jill's when she was a young girl.'

☉☉◎

Both Rose and Melissa sat in companionable silence as they read the story from start to finish. It didn't give much away, only that police assumed that Louise had run away with friends or an unknown boyfriend, and that her mother – while worried – was keeping up a steady watchdog petition around the area.

After the initial story, there were just small snippets in a few later newspapers that had been published, with the last appearance seeming to be in May, when a lack of leads or information caused the story to dry up.

Buoyed a little by their discovery, though frustrated with the lack of conclusion, it was Melissa that finally spoke.

'So, we know that it's probably Louise that Suzie is seeing in her dreams. I mean, it makes sense. So, why don't we print the photograph of the girl from the paper and take it down to that charity shop and see if they recognise her or the story? You never know, maybe they met her, or maybe her mum?'

With Rose in agreement, Melissa printed the articles from the local paper, and they headed off from the library down the main street to the charity shop where Rose had first purchased the clothes. Heading towards the shop, Melissa felt a strange, ominous sense of dread. It was here that the whole thing had begun, and though they didn't know why or even what was really happening, it felt like this charity shop might hold more information than they could even imagine.

'This is it,' Rose said, stopping outside a very ordinary-looking charity shop. It was a local shop rather than the large nationwide chain stores you normally see on high streets, raising money to support charities.

Rose and Melissa walked in, and straight away Melissa was a little taken aback. She hadn't known what to expect, but some of the shelves and rails looked almost trendy. Nothing like the charity shops she had ever been in before. She recalled their local charity shops up in Leeds, with clothes mixed up and a distinct musty smell that never really seemed to go away. This one, on the other hand, was well furnished, all colour co-ordinated clothes on rails and seemed really up to date; Melissa was genuinely impressed.

But now was not the time. They had a job to do.

Rose was already at the counter, asking for the lady who had served her. She couldn't recall her name, and so seemed to be describing her to the slightly bemused-looking older woman behind the till.

'She was slim, dark brown, short hair – obviously dyed but very well, I must say. I would say she was about fifty or sixty, so it can't have been that dark on its own, can it?' She laughed nervously. 'Anyway, she wasn't very tall; maybe 5'4"?'

The woman behind the counter shifted awkwardly, looking at Rose with a look that resembled both pity and a hint of skepticism.

'I'm really sorry, Madam, but the lady you are describing died about a year ago.' Her voice softened; 'How long ago was it you came in to the shop?'

Melissa, catching onto the woman's tone, realised she was humouring Rose. She must think Rose was going a little mad – and truth be told, Melissa could understand why. The older woman did seem to be struggling more and more with the revelations that were coming to light as the days went on. Maybe this was all becoming too much for Rose.

'It was about a week or so ago now and so it simply can't be the same lady, I'm sorry. Don't you have anyone else here with a description like that? She could have been in her forties, I suppose, or a little taller…' Rose tailed off uncertainly, clearly wracking her brain as she tried to recollect her previous visit to the shop.

'Hang on a minute. I'll just get Joanne in the back to speak to you. She's worked here for nearly ten years, so let's see what she says,' said the lady behind the till kindly. Melissa touched Rose's arm lightly and felt her stiffen a little.

The lady went to get Joanne, and when she came back through, Rose described the lady again. But just like the first time, Joanne told them that she was sorry, but the only lady with that description died a year previously.

'But that doesn't make sense,' Rose said, partly to herself and partly to Melissa, shaking her head.

'First, I get a lady giving me clothes to buy, even though I hadn't picked them up myself, and now here you are telling me the same lady died at least a year ago. I just don't understand.'

'Another thing,' added Joanne as they were about to leave. 'We don't actually sell underwear or nightwear. As you say, it's not something anyone would ever think to pick up in a charity shop, and we know it wouldn't sell.'

◎◎◎

'Come on, Rose, I'll treat you to a coffee,' Melissa said as they exited the shop onto the sunny high street. Inside the shop had felt a little dark by the time they left, and not just because they hadn't been in the sunlight. The whole thing was a little too weird for Melissa's liking. 'Let's go to that one where you can sit outside.'

So, they both headed off to Bee's Knee's. The weather was lovely, and Melissa figured they could spend some time discussing what had just happened. She felt a little embarrassed for Rose if truth be told, and wanted to give her a chance to mull over their experience in the charity shop before they got back to Jill and Suzie.

'You sit down, Rose; I'll get you a latte. That's what you have, isn't it?' she asked, pulling her purse from her pocket.

'Yes, love, thanks.' Rose sat herself down at one of the tables outside the deli coffee bar, her mind racing with what they'd just told her in the shop. She knew she hadn't got the wrong shop, and she knew she wasn't remembering the woman wrong. She knew it. But, she had to admit, what had happened just now didn't explain anything. Rather, it seemed to complicate things further.

Melissa brought back their coffees and sat down opposite Rose.

'Right, let's get to the bottom of this. Here's what we know: there is limited information in the papers, barely anything more we can learn from the library, and nobody knows anything about the lady who served you at the charity shop. Well, except for thinking she's now dead.' Melissa exhaled. 'We could always have a word with the police?' she added, glancing at Rose.

'Yes, I've been thinking the same,' said Rose. 'But even if they do have something on their file, it's not like they just hand out information whenever people ask for it.'

'No, I suppose you're right.' Melissa was stumped. What else could they do?

'We'll go to the police when we have a bit more information. Do any of those papers give the girl's name?' asked Rose.

Melissa looked through quickly. 'It's given her first name, it's Louise and her mum's called Sarah Crabtree.' She continued turning the pages over in her hands, scanning the limited information provided.

'Oh, hang on, it's got here she lives in the Bainbridge area. Do you know that area, Rose?'

'Yes, I do. It's about fifteen minutes by car or thirty minutes on the bus from my house. I've not really been to that area much, but, by all accounts, it's a nice little town – not too busy or anything.'

'Come on then,' said Melissa with a newfound vigor as she downed the rest of her coffee. 'Let's get home and see how Suzie is. Maybe she'd be up for a little trip to Bainbridge...'

Rose finished her drink, and the two of them headed off back to the car, which was parked back in the library car park.

24

'We're home,' called Rose as she and Melissa arrived home, desperate to share what they had learned.

'Shh, Mum. Suzie's asleep again.' Jill's head appeared around the living room door.

'Sorry love, how's she been?' Rose asked, lowering her voice as she followed Jill into the living room.

'To be honest, I'm really worried about her. As soon as she wakes up again, I'll get her to write down everything, then let her change into some other clothes as quickly as possible. She woke up a couple of hours ago after writhing about again. I left her alone for as long as I dared, but it was hard. She seemed so distressed. Then she woke herself up, and after talking to her, she managed to scribble something down. I can't really make out all the words on my own... I thought we could go through it all when she wakes up.

'Do you want me to have a quick look now,' offered Melissa, aware that the years spent next to Suzie in various class-rooms at school had given her an unfair advantage when it came to making out her friends' scruffy handwriting.

Jill picked up the writing pad from the coffee table and handed it to Melissa to read through.

Melissa went to sit outside in the warm heat of the garden and started sifting through the pages. She had to admit, it was fairly indecipherable, even by Suzie's standards.

Watching Melissa out the window, Jill turned to Rose. 'How did you get on today then, Mum?'

Picking up a fresh cup of tea, Rose relayed the whole story to her daughter, from going to the library and finding the papers to the non-existent lady at the charity shop.

'Bizarre,' said Jill, shaking her head in disbelief. She wasn't sure whether or not she should be worried about her mum. She had never shown any signs of confusion before now – in fact, she barely even acted like the older woman she was – but over the past few days, Jill had noticed a shift in her mother's confidence. She looked up and noticed Rose was watching her warily.

'Yes, I know. I'm not going mad, though, Jill. You have to believe me. Melissa believed me, but I could tell the lady behind the counter thought I was losing it, and I couldn't bear it.' Rose looked close to tears.

'I know,' Jill sighed. 'But put yourself in her shoes, Mum, would you believe her?'

'I suppose not,' laughed Rose a little shakily. 'Anyway, at my age I suppose I'm too old to care about what people think of me.'

As the women continued talking, and Melissa kept her head down inside the notebook, Suzie was starting to move about again, restless and agitated. Only, this time, the only sound she emitted was a faint murmuring, and it took a minute for Jill to realise that her daughter was finally waking up. She was relieved to see that, for once, Suzie looked fairly peaceful as she opened her eyes.

'Hi love,' Jill went to sit beside her as she started to sit up. 'Are you okay? How are you feeling?'

'Okay, I think.' Suzie rubbed her eyes and looked at her mum.

'I feel fine. It was… surreal. Don't get me wrong, it started bad, awful, in fact. The same as before. When I fell asleep,

I wasn't going into the house like before. He already had me – we were arguing at the top of the stairs, both falling down them, I try to get away but he's right behind me. I manage to get into the kitchen but he pushes me to the floor, hitting my head on a corner unit and that's when it goes dark. That's usually when I wake up, except this time I didn't wake up, the darkness lifted, and in my dream, I came round, and I was with a lady and an elderly couple. I guess it's the girl's mum and grandparents. I didn't recognise them, but SHE recognised them, you know? Anyway, I was with them, following them, but I wasn't talking to them. They didn't look at me or talk to me – it was like I wasn't there.'

Suzie swallowed hard. 'The adults were upset, but the two women were kind of smiley-sad, hugging each other a lot. It was like the nearer I got to them, they seemed more at ease, but they didn't see me. It was pretty weird actually, I tried to get their attention, but I couldn't. So, the dream carried on like that really, and then suddenly we were by the sea. The younger woman threw this big ring of flowers into the water, and the girl – me, I suppose – just walked away. Like everything was calmer now... I'm not sure I'm explaining it right. I don't really understand, but it was like a goodbye.'

As she finished her story, Suzie looked over to the window and noticed the magpie sitting on the patio step. It was looking straight at her. 'It's there again, Mum, look,' whispered Suzie, pointing towards it. 'Every time I have this dream, I wake up and see that magpie sitting on the window ledge or nearby. It has to be the same one!' she looked at her mother animatedly.

'Yes, love, I think your right. Maybe best to write your dream down while you remember it love?' As she began to scribble down everything she had just said, Suzie paused. This time it felt different – SHE felt different. Like she should take a little more time and tell it right. Putting pen to paper, she started writing again just as Melissa walked back in and sat down beside her.

As the girls sat in companionable silence, Suzie writing her story, Rose went into the kitchen to start making them something to eat. Jill sat with Suzie and Melissa, watching for a while until she could think of nothing else. 'Do you think you had better go and get changed out of those pyjamas now, love? I think you've been through enough today. We'll have something to eat and then we can discuss what happened today. We can't do anything before tomorrow, and then when we do...'

'What do you mean "do anything",' Suzie interrupted, looking up.

'Well, I mean, do we go see the girl's family, or do we go to the police?'

'Woah, stop right there, Mum. What exactly have you lot been up to today while I've been sleeping? Look, let's have our dinner, yes, but we need to discuss everything you've seen and done. Also, we don't know where the girl or her family live.'

Jill nodded, then went into the kitchen to help Rose with the dinner, though her mother seemed to have everything under control. Jill leaned against the counter and couldn't help but feel a little lost – just for a moment. No one needed her right now, Suzie had looked at her quite firmly when she suggested the next steps, and Jill knew her daughter would be stubborn in her thoughts on the matter. There was nothing she could do there right now, and now she couldn't even help with dinner. Lost in thought, she almost didn't notice Rose walking over to her and place a hand on her shoulder.

'You go make sure Suzie's okay, and love? Don't forget Melissa. She must be feeling a bit out of it at the moment too. Ask her if she wants to call her mum about staying on a bit longer… although she might not want to let on what's happening, or her mum might want her home.'

Jill went back in to sit with the girls while Rose finished off dinner.

'Have you spoken to your mum yet, Melissa?'

'No, I better go phone her before we eat, actually. How long do you think we will be staying for?' Melissa asked, not sure if she should be asking Suzie or Jill. She didn't want to outstay her welcome.

'To be honest, love, I'm not sure – it depends on how each day goes. If you want, tell your mum we'll be here another few days or so, and then we can always ring her again if it's going to be longer. Have you decided what you're going to say to her?'

'I'm just going to say the weather's great, we're having a great time, so we're all staying a bit longer. Trust me, Mum won't even question it.'

As Melissa went upstairs to fetch her phone and call her mum, Suzie went to get changed out of her pyjamas and into some jeans and a T-shirt. It felt good to wear something fresh and clean, and she immediately felt a little better as she stepped back downstairs – her mum beckoning her into the living room and over to the sofa.

'Here, love, come and sit with me for a few minutes while your gran's getting dinner sorted.'

Suzie sat on the settee next to her mum and leaned into her mum's arms. 'You know, Suzie, if this gets too much for you… we can just forget it and move on, go home. If that's what you want.'

'No, Mum, I need to get to the bottom of this. You were right. We do need to do something. Gran thinks I'm like her grandma, I know she does. And if that's the case, then what I'm seeing could really have happened, and I could be the only one who can sort it out. It's super freaky, I know, but I want to try my best to sort it out, or at least work out if it's true, before giving in.'

'I love you so much for that, sweetheart, and we're all here with you. You're not alone.'

'I think that's what's keeping me going, to be honest, Mum. I have you three. I couldn't do it on my own,' Suzie said honestly.

At that moment, Melissa appeared at the bottom of the stairs, and Rose's voice called through from the kitchen that dinner was ready. Their moment was over, but Jill felt better knowing she had given her daughter every option she could. Suzie wanted to carry on and get to the bottom of this, and Jill was proud of her. Jill gave Suzie another hug, and they both got up and walked across to the dining table.

Suzie drew in a huge breath, savouring the smell of fresh lasagne as it came out of the oven. 'Mmm smells lovely gran, you know lasagne is my favourite! You're the best.'

'Oh lovey, you sound just like you did when you were ten years old.'

Everyone laughed, and with the atmosphere a little lighter, they all sat down to eat.

'You know, since I've taken those pyjamas off and put my own clothes on, I feel suddenly so much more awake. I felt really drained and drowsy with the PJs on,' Suzie commented, digging into a piece of garlic bread.

'I can imagine a lot of energy goes into your dreams, but at least you can relax for a while,' Jill added thoughtfully. 'I'll wash the pyjamas again, and then you can decide what to do next. Maybe we need to consider burning them or putting them in the rubbish bin for good,' she suggested.

'Or maybe wear them again...' Suzie offered, looking at her mum.

'Could you make out what Suzie had written, Melissa?' asked Rose, changing the subject.

'Most of it, yes, but to be honest, I think Suzie is best looking at it herself and seeing if there is anything missing.'

'Where is it, Melissa? I can have a quick look now while I'm eating my tea.'

'Right then,' said Jill, a little louder than she intended. She didn't want the meal to be ruined but could already feel it spiralling out of her control. 'I need to know what you want to do, Suzie. A lot happened today with your grandma and Melissa, so we need to know where to go from here.'

Rose jumped in and told Suzie how they'd got on at the library and the charity shop.

Suzie listened and found that she wasn't really surprised with the outcome. After all, nothing else made sense, so why should this? Everything had been so normal a week ago, but now it seemed like her whole world had been turned upside down. Suzie was beginning to realise that she had a gift – whether it was a good gift or a bad gift, she wasn't sure yet, but its intention seemed clear enough. She could communicate through, and help, deceased people.

'You know Suzie,' added Jill, 'have you thought that she – the girl – might not even be... you know... deceased. I've been thinking this afternoon, and I really do think we should find out where the girl's mum and grandparents live. We should go and see them. It's the only way to know for sure.'

'That's what we thought today as well,' said Rose looking at Melissa, who nodded slowly.

'What do you want to do, Suzie?' Jill asked. 'And like I said earlier, if it's all getting too much, we can stop this now.' Suzie felt all eyes on her.

She smiled at her mum. 'You know we can't stop now, Mum. I want to help.' The smile faded from her face as she continued. 'I've got this gut feeling that something terrible happened to this girl, that she could even be the missing girl that Gran and Melissa read about. So yes, I think it's a good idea to go and see the girl's family.' She hesitated before continuing, aware that the next part of what she had to say would probably shock them.

'There's one other thing I want to do first, though, and that's go and see that guy working at the paper stand – you know, on Oxford Street. I want to just show him the photo you have and see what he does.'

By this point, no one was really eating; rather, they were just playing with their food, lost in their own individual thoughts.

'Right, come on you lot,' said Rose, breaking the silence. 'I know you must be hungry, so let's eat up, and then we can discuss what we are going to do tomorrow to help Suzie do what she wants to do.' At that, everyone continued eating their dinner, and the conversation slowly settled into an uneasy truce – discussing the weather and mundane things like what else Rose could grow in her garden.

☉☉☉

But Suzie couldn't concentrate. As Melissa asked Rose about the growth time of different vegetables, Suzie got up and went over to the sideboard, picking up the paper cuttings before sitting back at the table to finish her dinner. She started poring over the cuttings and was silent for a few minutes until she saw the photo.

She dropped her fork, her hand slowly rising to her mouth.

Her eyes wide, she looked at the photo, then at her mum, and back at the photo.

'Oh my God,' said Suzie slowly.

'It's the same girl, isn't it... the same girl as in your dream?' said Rose, eyeing her as Melissa watched on intently.

'Yes. I mean, I think I knew it was going to be... but seeing it in print... it makes it real.' Looking up with a resolve in her eyes, Suzie was adamant. 'The guy at the magazine stand, we have to show him this. His face will tell us if he knows the girl in the photograph or not. I know it's him.'

Jill reached for the photograph and, for the first time, properly looked at the face smiling out from the paper. The face of a young girl with so much kindness, so much to live for and so much still to come. If she was honest with herself, she was terrified of what they were going to find out.

'She's so bonny,' piped up Rose. 'Not that different from you two girls. She would have had the same interests, music, boyfriends...' she trailed off, touching the photograph softly. They were all thinking the same thing, that whatever had happened to this girl was a loss far greater than anything they had previously imagined.

'You're the one that's seen it all, Suze... do you think Louise is still alive?' Rose asked, using Louise's name for the first time. Now that they knew who she was, it felt right to use her name.

'I'd like to think she is,' Suzie replied honestly.

After dinner, when all the washing up and drying had been done, they congregated in the living room.

'First of all, Suzie,' started Jill, 'It's time for you to have a good night's sleep ready for tomorrow. You should wear your own pyjamas.'

'Yes, I was thinking that anyway,' Suzie agreed, much to Melissa's relief.

'Right then, that's settled. Now, Suzie, you're the one in control here. What do you want to do tomorrow?' asked Rose.

'Well, I'm totally out of my depth with this, but I would like to see the girl's mum and her grandparents – if that even is who they are. They might be able to help me – us. Until I've seen the girl's parents… well, I can't really think beyond that.'

'That seems fair enough, love. What do you think?' Jill asked, turning to both Melissa and Rose, who nodded encouragingly.

'I mean, for all I know,' Suzie continued, 'when we go round there, the girl might be with her mum and dad – really happy. The guy might just be a weird Uncle, and everyone might be living happily together.'

'Yes, you're right… the only thing is, maybe just you two should go.' Rose indicated Jill and Suzie, glancing apologetically at Melissa. 'Can you imagine if we all turned up… they would think we were crazy.'

They all laughed, and after a concerned glance from Suzie, Melissa wholeheartedly agreed. It should be Suzie and her mum.

⊙◉◎

By the time their plan was drawn out, it was 7.50pm – far too early for bed but a little too late to start any new activities. Suzie and Melissa decided to head to the local, with a little encouragement from Jill, who desperately wanted her daughter and her friend to enjoy a little time together on their holiday.

The girls, realising they couldn't be bothered to get changed just to go to the local, decided to go as they were; Suzie throwing her hair up and Melissa plaiting hers before adding a little lippy. At last, thought Jill as the door closed behind them. Suzie looks like she doesn't have a care in the world.

And with that, she turned and went to get a bottle of wine for her and Rose.

'It's nice to see a smile on Suzie's face.'

'Yes, I was thinking the same,' smiled Rose.

'Do you really think we're doing the right thing, digging all this up? After all, it was just a dream, and we're relying a lot on Suzie's hunch…' Jill said, finally feeling able to voice her concerns with the girls safely out of the house.

Rose smiled again, a little sadly this time. 'Yes, love, I think we have to. There are things happening here that are out of our control, and for some reason, Suzie is in the thick of it. Suzie has a gift – that I'm sure of, Jill, whether we like it or not. We should encourage her to express more and bring it out. When I read my grandma's notebook, it is so obvious that she wished she had somebody who she could trust to tell. Not just the cases but everything. That's why it's good we're here for Suzie.'

The adults talked and talked, retelling stories of their family, old holidays together and laughing until it grew dark. It felt good to laugh.

Meanwhile, the girls were finally letting themselves relax into the holiday, drinking cider and eyeing up the local talent.

'I can't believe you like him!' cried Suzie glancing across at the guy who Melissa had just revealed she had the hots for. 'I mean, come on, you can do better than that!' Melissa nudged her friend hard.

'You know me, Suzie, I like a bit of rough.'

'You can say that again. Hey up, he's looking over,' Suzie giggled as Melissa blushed. 'Look over, Mel, it's what you wanted!'

The guy caught Melissa's eye, and as he winked, Suzie beckoned him over with her most serious of expressions.

Before Melissa could argue, he was picking up his drink and making his way toward their table.

As he came over, with Melissa distracted, Suzie took the opportunity to take in her surroundings and enjoy the feeling of freedom.

Glancing across at the bar, she suddenly felt a knot in her throat which made her simultaneously gulp at her cider, dissolve into a coughing fit, and claw at Melissa's jacket.

As she continued to watch, her breathing came more steadily as she cleared her throat and took a few deep breaths. The very man from the magazine stand stood and made his way back towards a woman who sat at a small table a few feet from the bar, partly concealed by a large potted plant. She couldn't tell, but it didn't look like anyone from her dream. From her position, Suzie was sure he couldn't see her, but she still drew away a little, tapping Melissa on the shoulder.

Melissa swatted her away at first, engaged in conversation with the guy who had winked at them – whose name turned out to be Paul – before eventually turning to face her. 'What, Suzie?'

'Look! At the bar, the guy there, it's him.' As Paul eyed the two of them, Suzie wished he would go away. She needed to keep an eye on the paperstand man, and Paul was blocking her view.

'Hey, are you okay?' Paul asked Suzie, the first words he had spoken directly to her. It seemed that he had caught on to the fact that she wasn't interested in chatting and only had eyes for Melissa.

'What? Sorry no, it's just I've got things on my mind.'

Shrugging, Paul asked the girls if they would like to join him and his mates, and after a stern and persuasive look from Melissa, Suzie gave in, and they obliged. All the time, Suzie kept an eye on the paperstand guy.

The lads who were with Paul were talkative and seemed friendly enough, and despite her distraction, Suzie didn't want to ruin this for Melissa. She had ruined her holiday enough. After about half an hour, Suzie looked over again towards the paperstand guy; alarmed to see that he was no longer there. The woman was gone too.

'I can't believe that,' said Suzie in Melissa's ear. 'That guy has left with that woman.'

'Well, you had plenty of time to go over to him if you wanted to,' Melissa retorted, a little irritated at Suzie's lack of interest in the group around them. It was coming across as quite rude now.

'No, but I wanted to follow him and see where he lived. I just hope that woman's okay...' she tailed off, and Melissa immediately felt bad that she had snapped at her friend. Plus, she really was feeling quite tipsy now.

'I'm sure she's okay!' said Melissa, a little more confidently than she felt.

Suzie smiled at her friend, realising now that Melissa had perhaps had a few too many. She hadn't drunk that much herself, her head was too full of what was going to happen tomorrow.

At 11.40pm, Suzie decided it was time to call it a night. 'Come on Melissa, we need to go home now. Make your arrangements to see Paul again and let's go.'

'Yes, okay, I'm coming.' Melissa was giggling, handing Paul her number as he promised to ring her. He really was quite sweet, Suzie decided as he said goodbye to her friend, offering to take the girls home. But Suzie declined. She didn't want anyone to know where her grandma lived or where they were staying.

Melissa talked non-stop all the way home to Rose's house. Suzie was pleased, Paul had seemed nice, and she was glad her friend had had a good night. Suzie just wished she herself was in a better mood too. A couple of the guys that were with him had seemed pretty decent.

'Oh, he is so gorgeous, don't you think, Suzie?' asked Melissa, linking arms with her friend. 'Do you think he will ring me?'

'Yes, of course he will. Why wouldn't he?'

Melissa just shrugged her shoulders in an over-the-top drunken way. 'Don't know! Come on, let's get home.'

It didn't take them long to walk home to Rose's house, and as they approached the door, Suzie pulled the keys out of her bag and let them both in. Turning to Melissa, she put a finger over her lips, asking, 'I'm going to make us a hot drink. Do you want one?'

'Mmmm,' mumbled Melissa.

Suzie made hot chocolate, and the girls sat in the ki.alking about Paul, and Paul, oh... and Paul again. Suzie had never seen her friend so infatuated with a lad so quickly. But, she supposed, Melissa was drunk, and she knew her friend could become quite attached. She wished she could feel a little more elated herself.

After Suzie had finished her hot chocolate and listened to Melissa for long enough, she suggested they go to bed. It was now going on 1.30 in the morning, and they had a lot on the next day.

'Come on, Melissa, we won't get up before lunch at this rate. Let's get off to bed,' she said, pulling Melissa up from the chair.

'Good idea, I can dream about Paul then.'

Suzie just laughed. 'I hope something comes of this you know, Melissa. You are so hooked on him. You haven't been like this about anyone in ages!' laughed Suzie.

'Bring it on,' said Melissa, winking as they made their way up the stairs, and as they both laughed, they momentarily forgot about the sleeping adults upstairs.

But Jill wasn't asleep.

From the other side of the door, she could hear the girls laughing – but she wasn't annoyed. If anything, she was happy Suzie was laughing. She'd not heard her laugh much since they'd arrived some five days earlier, and it was time they all enjoyed themselves a little.

25

The rest of the night passed peacefully enough, and by the time the sun rose the next morning, both Suzie and Melissa felt as if they had actually had a decent night's sleep – though Melissa's face was anything but peaceful.

'Morning Mel, Mel, how you feeling?' Suzie grinned over at her friend.

'Oh, my god. I feel... Suze, did I show myself up last night? I feel a bit rough this morning,' Melissa admitted.

'No, you were fine... but you were all over that Paul.'

'Who? Oh, him, yes he was alright. Actually, he was pretty fit, don't you think?' She looked hopefully at her friend.

'Not my type but you seemed pretty keen!' At that, Melissa pulled the cover over her head and let out a loud groan which made Suzie laugh out loud.

'Oh no, I didn't, did I? Did I come across as desperate?'

Suzie pulled back the cover and sat in front of Melissa, smiling a little as she said, 'He's taken your number and said he will phone you.'

Far from making her feel better, Melissa groaned again. 'So that obviously means he won't. Not that I'm bothered... really, I just want to forget last night, take some painkillers and have a coffee.' She knew she wasn't really fooling Suzie, but her friend had the decency to nod and cease all talk on the subject, letting the two of them get dressed in companionable silence. Melissa's mind was racing over the events of the previous evening, while Suzie could think of nothing except the day ahead.

The girls were up and dressed in no time, and as they made their way downstairs, they just caught the tail end of Jill and Rose's conversation, making plans and predictions about what they would find out that day.

'Right then, love, what time do you want to leave? Are you still happy for me to come with you...?' Jill felt a little like she was treading on eggshells, but the last thing she wanted to do at this stage was let her daughter feel uncomfortable with the situation. She knew there was a fine line between Suzie's love of her mother and the bond she had with her best friend, and Jill would understand if Suzie would rather take Melissa – even if, inside, it would hurt her more than she let on.

Suzie, however, nodded decidedly – and Jill let out a sigh of quiet relief as her daughter said, 'Oh yes, Mum, we need to go soon. I was actually thinking, I might wear those pyjamas again tonight... you know, if it does turn out that she died. You never know, once we know, I might be able to find out where her body is. That way, at least we can go to the police and let them know.'

Jill was puzzled. 'What do you mean "where her body is"?' She looked over at her own mother questioningly; 'I'm assuming they've found her body?'

Rose just shrugged. 'Think of the papers, dear. There was nothing in there about a body.'

'Yes,' nodded Suzie, 'and they don't know who did it. It's all a massive mystery, but maybe I can help solve it.'

'I know the papers said the trail was going thin, but that was months ago. Maybe they've found her now,' said Jill, a note of hesitation in her voice.

'Well, that's another reason why we have to go see Louise's family then, isn't it?' hit back Suzie defiantly.

It was decided that Melissa and Rose would stay at home until Jill and Suzie got back – or at least until they phoned with an update. Rose couldn't bear to leave the house in case her daughter and granddaughter needed her, and Melissa could barely think straight, let alone bring herself to go anywhere.

Just before they walked out the door, Suzie made a split-second decision to run upstairs and grab the pyjamas, stuffing them into her bag under her purse. At least if she had them close, it was something to show the family... maybe they could tell her if the pyjamas really had belonged to Louise, she thought hopefully. She knew, one way or another, today she would finally get some answers.

Jill jumped in the car and thinking aloud, said to Suzie, now sat in the passenger seat 'So, first of all we need to go to the library and see if we can find that girl's address.'

Suzie tutted. 'The girl has a name, Mum. Louise. I feel like I know her,' she added, glancing out the window.

Jill turned to face her daughter briefly before putting the car into first gear and pulling out of the drive. 'I know, love. I think to some extent we all feel a little like we know her. I just... as soon as I think of her name, it becomes so much more real. So much harder to contemplate. I just thought maybe it would be easier for all of us...'

But Suzie shook her head. 'It's Louise.'

Ten minutes later they pulled up outside the library; Suzie barely waiting for the car to stop before she jumped out and made for the entrance. Taking the paper cuttings out of her bag, Jill followed, and the two of them were soon flicking through phone books relating to the various boroughs of Greater London. One or two strange glances were thrown their way, likely by strangers who thought the phone books were outdated and pointless, but Jill and Suzie both knew it was the quickest way to find the information they needed.

As they searched, Suzie broke the silence with something she had been thinking about since the previous night in the bar. 'You know, Mum, we saw that guy again from the paperstand in the bar last night. I was wondering, maybe he lives locally to Grandma?'

'Keep looking and let's see, you take this one,' Jill passed one of the thick books to Suzie before picking up another one for herself. 'I'll take this one. What's the surname of Louise's family?'

'Crabtree,' Suzie said absentmindedly as her eyes scanned the pages. That was the surname of her mum anyway that they gave out in the local paper and her first name is Sarah.'

'Do we know what Sarah's parents' surname is?' Jill asked. 'After all, they went to stay with Louise's grandparents, didn't they?'

I don't know. Let's start with Crabtree. Surely we will come across someone whose related to them.'

Silence fell as both Suzie and Jill looked through the phone books, scanning every listing of Crabtree and writing down the details of them all. By the time they had looked through all five phone books, Suzie had twenty-two possible phone numbers, and Jill had just fourteen.

Right, come on. Let's go grab a coffee and start ringing round,' Suzie said, grabbing her bag and scrambling to her feet, followed closely by Jill. It was hard to contain the sense of achievement they felt after their success of the past hour, and it was with some jubilation that they settled down at an outside table at the local café and ordered iced coffees.

Pulling out their phones both Jill and Suzie got straight to work, calling the numbers on the lists. The first one Jill called went straight to voicemail and so didn't leave a message. The second number Jill called couldn't help and the third put the phone down on her, that's how it continued for both of them. That was until Suzie having got halfway through her list called the next number and, after five rings, was about to give up when she heard a click and a voice at the other end saying very quietly, 'Hello?'

Startled for a minute thinking it was just another call she was going to have to abort, panicked and handed the phone to her mum knowing she would approach the situation better than she ever could. Jill who in turn desperately wished she had considered in advance how best to approach the delicate subject.

'Hello! Is that Mrs. Crabtree? You don't know me, but I was wondering... do you have a daughter by the name of Louise?' She hated herself for the bluntness of her delivery, but found that when it came to it, she didn't know what else she could possibly say.

'Who wants to know?' asked the quiet voice.

'Well, like I say, you don't know me, but I think I have... sorry, I don't really know how to put it. I think there might be a connection between Louise and my daughter, Suzie.' Holding her breath, there was silence for a moment before the voice spoke again – only this time, the quiet and timid voice was gone, replaced by a hardness Jill hadn't expected.

'Look, if this is a prank joke, it's pretty sick. You're sick. Just leave me alone, please!' and before Jill could say anything, the voice was cut off, and the phone beeped. The woman, Sarah Crabtree, had hung up.

'I don't know what to do, Suze. I think that was her. It must have been. Oh, she sounded so upset... she just put the phone down!' Jill couldn't forget the distinct wobble she had heard in the woman's voice – a wobble which cut right through the harsh tone and spoke of her obvious pain.

'Well, we've got to try again; it's obviously the right family!' Suzie said animatedly. 'Well done, Mum! She's probably just so fed up with the papers and everyone calling her... I wouldn't worry! You look so worried! It does make you wonder, I guess, why she doesn't just change her telephone number and go ex-directory,' she pondered this final thought, thinking about what it would take to make the media go away.

'Maybe she's worried that if she did that, Louise wouldn't be able to contact her again. Let's face it, everyone can remember a landline number if they've had it for years but you never remember mobile numbers because you just dial by the name and it's automatic,' Jill filled the silence quietly, knowing exactly that if it was her, she'd never stop waiting for Suzie to come home.

'Yes, you're right. I didn't think of that,' nodded Suzie.

Suddenly it all felt very real, and she knew, just like Mrs. Crabtree, they couldn't give up.

'You must try again, Mum. We have to sort this out. I know they're angry and upset, and she might have said she didn't want to listen, but when they do listen to us, they will understand what we're trying to do.'

So, Jill tried calling again, and again – but it just kept ringing.

'No joy,' said Jill, finally putting her phone down. 'She obviously knows it's us.'

Suzie thought for a moment, knowing it was the only way. 'Well then, there's only one thing for us to do. We will have to just call round and see them. We need her address?'

Jill shook her head cautiously – unsure if this was the right thing to do. It felt so intrusive... but how else could they help? She knew they had no choice.

'We can get it from the phone book, can't we?'

'You stay here,' said Suzie to her mum, 'I'll run round to the library and get it.' And before Jill could argue, Suzie was gone.

Running through the library door, Suzie desperately tried to recall which book they had found the right Louise in. Flicking through the phone books, she finally identified the one with the number she had scribbled on her hand and wrote down the address of Louise's family before dashing back to the cafe.

As she slumped back in her seat, Suzie gave the address to Jill, who typed it quickly into her phone. '102 Waters Crescent, Basingstoke. Suzie laughed, why didn't I think of that and take my mobile with me to the library, noting the address like you've just done,' shaking her head. 'Don't suppose you know the area do you, Mum?'

'You're not thinking straight love, that's all and unfortunately, I don't know the area love, but we'll just use the sat nav in the car. We can go by that.'

Suzie felt a prickle of trepidation – or was it excitement? – coursing through her. They were so close now. Finally, she might be about to understand what all this meant.

Getting back into the car a few minutes later, Jill reached for the sat nav and quickly programmed in the address.

'Oh my God, it's only twenty minutes away. She lives that near to us!'

'Do you think that's how I got involved as well? Because I'm staying with Grandma, and it's so near to her?'

Jill thought about it for a moment before shaking her head. 'No, love, I think it's just a coincidence. I think if you can help this girl, you can help anyone – regardless of where they live.'

Suzie nodded before turning to focus on the road ahead.

'Come on, Mum, let's get on with it. I can't deal with this for much longer. I mean... I know it's going to be hard for them, what I'm going to tell them... Oh god, what if I can't do it? Tell me honestly, Mum, if it was you, and you knew something had happened to me, would you want to know what had happened? Would it help you to feel more at peace?'

Her eyes bore into Jill with an intensity that Jill hadn't seen on her daughter's face very often. She was growing up.

'Yes, love, I would want to find out exactly what had happened and who was responsible. At peace, I'm not sure love, but I would need to know.'

26

The neighbourhood where the Crabtree's lived was an area that would be described as "quaint and traditional", with whitewashed houses which looked like they had been built in the 1920s and cared for with a good level of upkeep and maintenance.

Jill and Suzie entered the street at number 188, parking and walking almost to the centre before they finally reached number 102. The two of them walked in silence, aware that there was nothing to be said at that moment. Suzie found that the excitement that had filled her had now dissipated, replaced by worry and the gravity of what was about to happen. Jill couldn't get the voice of the woman, demanding they leave her alone, out of her head.

As they approached the front door, Jill held Suzie back and said she would do the talking first – not wanting the woman to slam her front door right in Suzie's face. Though reluctant at first, Suzie agreed that it was best her mother speak first and explain the situation, before letting her jump in.

Knocking on the door, the two of them took a small step back as they heard footsteps approaching, unsure of the reception they were going to get when the door opened. Finally, the door swung open, and they were greeted by the sight of a woman – possibly in her mid to late forties.

The woman held herself well, though Suzie could tell from looking at her face that she had been crying. Her eyes were puffy; with a feeling of guilt, Suzie realised it was their call that had upset her. She swallowed and looked at her mum, suddenly glad that Jill had offered to speak first. Suzie had no idea what to say.

Luckily, the woman spoke first. 'Hello?' she questioned, looking at them warily.

'Mrs. Crabtree?' asked Jill. The woman just looked at them both, not saying a word. Jill continued, 'I… we're here to talk to you about Louise. Please forgive me for asking, but is Louise your daughter?'

The woman's eyes filled with tears – confirmation enough for both Jill and Suzie that this was indeed Sarah Crabtree. 'Are you the lady that phoned earlier?' she asked, her voice shaking.

Jill nodded and stretched out a hand, lightly holding the door as if to stop it from closing. 'Yes, but before you push us away, I promise we aren't here to hound you. We're not from the papers, God knows we don't know anything about media or television or anything. We want to help.'

Suddenly, at her final words, Mrs. Crabtree's eyes flared up with anger. 'I've told you folk to stay away with your ghost stories and voodoo nonsense. I'm not having it. I don't need you to talk to my daughter!' and with that, her voice raising a little at the finality of her words, she started to close the door – but Jill's firm hold withstood the force long enough for her to make one final plea.

'Sarah, please.'

At the use of her first name, Mrs. Crabtree's anger suddenly dissolved, and she stepped back – almost looking taken aback by her own force. Suzie looked on in horror as the woman before her, as quickly as she had stood firm, seemed to collapse in on herself. Jill continued, softer now.

'Please let us speak, just for five minutes. We'll explain everything we know about Louise's disappearance and about what my daughter here knows. This is Suzie,' she added, pushing Suzie forward slightly.

'I don't understand,' Mrs. Crabtree said, shaking her head in disbelief. 'The police have done all they can – there are no leads. There's nothing to know. We don't know if Louise disappeared or if she ran away...' she choked back a sob but continued anyway. 'I don't know you. I've never seen you before. I've never seen you with my daughter.' The last sentence was directed right at Suzie, who blushed.

This was not going to plan.

As she finished speaking, an older man appeared at her shoulder, putting his hand on Mrs. Crabtree's arm and stepping in front of her a little.

'I'm Louise's grandad. What is this about?'

'Please...' began Jill. 'Just give us five minutes. If you don't want to talk after that, we will leave, but please let my daughter tell you what she has to say.'

Silence hung in the air while the older man looked to his daughter. Eventually, she shrugged and stepped back, widening the door just a little and letting them in.

The sight that greeted Suzie and Jill was a well-kept house, clean, with fresh flowers in a vase on the table beside the door. They took off their shoes and followed Sarah into what must be the living room, her father right behind them. It was clear he was intent on protecting his daughter, and Jill couldn't blame him.

'Please, sit down.' Sarah gestured vaguely at the sofa. Sitting down, Jill inhaled and got ready to speak again, but before she could, the gentleman cut in.

'Mr. Crabtree,' he began, extending his hand. They both took it.

'Now, I don't know what it is you want, but my daughter here has been through enough. Don't go getting our hopes up if you're here to cause upset. In fact, if you are here for that, then you might as well just go now.'

Sarah cut him off, explaining, 'Dad used to do a lot for Louise. She had him wrapped around her little finger, didn't she, Dad?' she added fondly.

'We miss her terribly,' Mr. Crabtree finished before falling silent. The silence was clear – it was Jill and Suzie's turn.

Deciding to start on an even footing, Jill looked at Mr. Crabtree and asked, 'If you don't mind my asking, does your wife live here too?'

'She's at her sisters for the week, needed a break. We said we'd call her if there was any news… look, are you going to tell us what this is about or not?' Mr. Crabtree was losing patience, and Jill knew it was time to cut to the chase.

'All we ask is that you listen carefully and don't judge what we say until you've heard it all,' Jill said, looking at Suzie.

'It's my story, really,' Suzie began, aware that within the next few minutes, she was about to change everything…

27

'I guess I should start at the beginning,' began Suzie, sitting back in her chair a little. The atmosphere in the room was tense – she could almost see Sarah holding her breath – and she wanted more than anything to leave. But she knew she had to do this.

'About five days ago, we arrived here from Leeds to visit my grandma. My gran bought me some stuff in the charity shop – she often does when she knows we're visiting. She knows I like to make new stuff and turn dresses into tops and add extra elements...' she tailed off, realising she was going off on a tangent.

'Anyway, the clothes... there were some pyjamas in with the other stuff, and I think... I understand, they could be Louise's.'

With that, she picked up her bag and dug around, retrieving the pyjamas and handing them to Sarah, who took them with a shaking hand.

'Oh god. Yes, these are Louise's... but how...?'

'My gran was approached in the charity shop by a woman, at the time she thought it was an employee but when she went back, they said the lady didn't work there anymore. Gran didn't really want to buy the pyjamas, but the woman insisted, and Gran gave in – just to get rid of the woman more than anything. She didn't think anything of it, she was just going to throw them away if I didn't want them or take them back to the charity shop – it's pretty weird, to be honest, having pyjamas from a charity shop. But she washed them anyway and gave them to me.'

Jill held her daughter's hand as Suzie took a deep breath and continued. She knew she had their attention now, but it was about to get a lot harder.

'That's when it started.'

'What started?' asked Sarah urgently.

It took about ten minutes for Suzie to relay all the details from her dreams – starting with the first dream and ending with the additional scenes from her latest dream – and she was aware of every single second. The room was stifling, and she didn't think she could bear it much longer... the silence...

'Can you describe the man in your dreams?' Mr. Crabtree finally spoke, in hushed tones. Sarah looked shell-shocked but turned to Suzie and nodded at her father's question.

'Oh yes, actually, I can do better than that,' Suzie said, nodding back. 'I can tell you where he works. I – me and my friend Melissa – we saw him working on a paper stall outside Oxford Street tube station. He's got dark hair, quite wavy, probably mid-forties... oh, and he's got tattoos across his fingers.'

Another silence, and then, 'That's him. That's sounds like my ex-partner. I left him at the time my daughter went missing.' Sarah said, putting her head in her hands and started sobbing. It was heartbreaking to watch.

'Yes,' whispered Suzie.

'That's what the fight was about,' the woman said, pulling her hands away from her face.

'Can I ask... what did you fight about? What happened on that day?' Suzie asked, aware that she was probably crossing a boundary, but no longer able to hold it in. She knew now that what she had seen had been real, but she was no closer to understanding why it had happened.

'His name is Andy,' Sarah began, 'he was my partner. A bit of a rebound maybe, after Louise's father and I split up...' she broke off. 'Andy was fun, he made me laugh at the start of our relationship, and he made me feel young. I thought he was alright, really. Yes, we argued, but at first it didn't matter – just silly things, really. But it got worse, and it was tearing me and Louise apart. She couldn't bear to see me upset. It probably reminded her of me and her dad before we split. I changed my surname back to my maiden name, Crabtree not long after and started a fresh.' Sarah started explaining. 'Anyway, she started spending more and more time here with her grandparents. I couldn't tell her, but I hated her living here with my mum and dad rather than with me. So much so that I decided to end it with Andy. My daughter had to come first. After picking Louise up from here after spending more time with her grandparents, we returned home and after another argument, decided to leave there and then. I packed some of our belongings and we left.'

She cleared her throat and looked around desperately, her eyes landing on a glass of water which she picked up and drained in one go. Her eyes were haunted, but her voice was strong as she continued.

'We came here, and Mum said she'd fix us dinner, we both thought everything was going to be okay. Louise though had left her mobile behind and so said she was going to go back for it, she was supposed to be seeing her friend Abi. I was happy for her to walk – it wasn't dark, it was only about 6pm, and her friend – Abi was just a fifteen-minute walk away. I texted her, probably about 7.30pm, just checking in really – telling her everything was going to be okay. She had been so worried about me... but she didn't reply. I wasn't worried then, I mean, she sometimes has her phone on silent, and if they were busy… well, it made sense. I still hadn't heard from her when I went up to bed, so I texted her about 11pm saying goodnight and telling her I loved her…'

She trailed off again, and Mr. Crabtree stepped in, Sarah resting her head in her hands as he continued the story.

'We decided to call Abi. We weren't worried, not really, but Sarah wanted to make sure Louise was with her and was ok. We called her, but Abi said she hadn't seen her – Louise had never arrived at her house. One thing Abi said… she said she'd received a text from Louise, sometime just before 8pm, saying she wasn't coming over anymore. She thought it was odd, but she knew about the move and figured that Louise was helping her mum out instead.'

He sighed heavily and put his arm around Sarah's shoulders. Jill's grip on Suzie's arm tightened.

'That's when we called the police,' continued Mr. Crabtree. 'But with the information – or lack of – and given Louise's age… there wasn't anything they could really do. She wasn't technically a missing person, at least not yet. So it was back to us.'

At this point, Sarah lifted her head and carried on. 'I tried all her friends I had contact numbers for and went out looking… the police didn't arrive until about 2.30am, and then when they did, all they said was that she was eighteen and perfectly entitled to do what she wanted. They did seem more interested when I said she had never turned up at her friend's house, though, and eventually they radioed in for a look out.'

When neither of them seemed to be ready to say any more, Suzie probed gently, 'Did they find anything?'

'Two days passed by and nothing – no sign. We sat by the phone waiting, our friends and neighbours were out looking, but there was nothing. It's like she just disappeared. The police searched a five-mile radius, dogs and everything, but there was no sign. That was when we decided to contact the local TV – the papers – anyone who would listen. They were good, but there wasn't enough information, and pretty soon the trail went cold.

'Our story – Louise's story – wasn't enough to keep people reading.' Sarah's voice was laced with disgust at this, and Jill's heart went out to her. To be told by money-grabbing media giants that her daughter wasn't a big enough story... Jill could only imagine the hurt.

'Oh, there were calls, make no mistake. Everyone wanted a piece of the action, but nothing solid. Nothing real,' Sarah's eyes swam with tears.

'I called Andy to check when Louise had called by the house as she'd obviously picked up her phone as she'd text Abi. He just said he'd not seen her. He went on to say that he was probably out when she'd called, after all she did have her own key and so I thought nothing more of it. He was very convincing and why would he lie?'

'Where is the house?' asked Jill, thinking that now was as good a time as any to cut to the chase.

'About twenty minutes walk away in the next village, Shilsdon or five minutes in the car. It's probably a right state, what with him living on his own now and all... but he's still there. As far as I know.'

'Do you think... could we go there? Have a look around?' Suzie asked hopefully. She knew that as soon as she walked in, she would know if it was the right house or not.

'Would you let a stranger in?' Sarah asked Suzie, a small smile on her face.

'No, I probably wouldn't,' admitted Suzie, respecting the irony of this statement, all too aware that she and her mother were strangers in this very home. 'But asking doesn't cost anything, does it? And if it means getting to the bottom of this... then I'm prepared to ask.'

Sarah nodded at this. 'You're right. Let me try him now. I mean, he didn't much care for Louise – always thought she was in the way – but he might help us, for me. God, I hope you're wrong about this,' she added.

'So do we,' admitted Jill. 'But Sarah, if it was me, I know I would want to know everything. No matter how farfetched. No matter how hard it is to take in.'

'Oh, I'm all nervous. I don't know what to say to him.'

At this, Suzie smiled a little, remembering Melissa the night before and how nervous she had been about speaking to Paul – the guy in the bar. If the situation they were in wasn't so serious, she would think Sarah was just a nervous teenager like them.

'It was always his house. We just lived there,' continued Sarah. 'I don't have any say or right to demand entry...'

At that, Jill had a sudden idea. 'Have you got anything left there, anything you could go to pick up? That might just get us in the door?'

'Oh yes! Some of Louise's clothes, I think... nothing I need really, but you could be on to something there.'

With that, Sarah rose from the armchair and crossed the living room to the hall, collecting her phone from the stand.

The phone rang – and rang; all of them waiting with bated breath. And when it seemed as if the phone was about to go to voicemail... a male voice broke the silence.

'Sarah?' Everyone could hear the other end. Immediately, Sarah realising the phone was on loudspeaker, took it off cutting the conversation down to just her end.

'I know you didn't really expect to hear from me again... not after our latest argument. But I was hoping you would let me come round and pick up the last of Louise's things?'

Silence as he responded. Sarah paled a little.

'Why not?' Sarah looked over at Jill and Suzie as she paused again, then, in a sterner voice, 'Well, it's okay, Andy, if you won't let me pick them up, then I'm sure the police will be happy to call round for me. After everything that's happened and all...'

Another pause, and then...

'Okay, great. I'll call round tomorrow then, say about 11ish? Okay, 12? See you then.' And with that, she hung up.

'We're going?' asked Suzie, barely daring to hope...

'Yes,' Sarah confirmed. 'But he wasn't happy. Said he would have to get someone to watch the stall for him.'

'Can I ask a question,' asked Jill, breaking Suzie's train of thought. 'What did you mean, just now, about your latest argument?'

Sarah shrugged. 'Oh, it was nothing, it's just... I've always known that Louise did go round to his place, even though he denies seeing her. Not just because of the text from Louise to her friend Abi but call it a mother's intuition... Anyway, I went round to have it out with him and he went ballistic – I mean really mad, and in the end I just got out of there and left. I did mention it to the police, but they just said they'd interviewed him and conducted a full search, and that he was clean.'

Her face etched with despair, she slumped back against her chair and finally allowed the tears to flow.

⊙⊙⊚

After another twenty minutes, when Jill suggested it was time they leave, Suzie couldn't have felt more relieved. The gravity of her revelation had hit home, and Sarah was inconsolable.

They agreed to meet back at the house at 11am the next day to travel to Andy's house together. Though unspoken, they all knew they needed the support of each other, and none of them – not even Mr. Crabtree – had an issue with car-sharing for the journey.

As her father saw Jill and Suzie to the door, Sarah let her mind wash over with a thought. She knew it was going to be a long journey, and in a way, part of her already knew what the outcome was. But she vowed, on that first day without Louise, that she wouldn't rest until she found her. No matter how bad things were going to be, she needed to know.

28

As they drove home, Jill and Suzie barely spoke – unable to voice all the emotions they had felt that day. Knowing they would have to relay the whole story to Rose and Melissa when they got home, it was like they'd reached an unspoken agreement to revel in their companionable silence for a little while longer.

As predicted, Rose and Melissa were waiting on tenterhooks, and Jill barely had time to pour a glass of water before the two of them were leaning in, and the questions began.

◉◉◉

By the time they had finished telling the story from their day, Jill felt drained. Suzie had remained quite quiet, only really chipping into the story when Jill couldn't remember a detail or reaction – it seemed like Suzie had them all memorised. Jill couldn't blame her for keeping to herself; it had been one hell of a day, and they both knew that tomorrow would be even more intense.

Upon hearing the plan for the next day, Rose immediately got up and started bustling around again, clearly distressed by the emotional depth of the story and the uncertainty which faced them. After that, when they could discuss it no more, the rest of the day seemed to pass by without event.

As the day wore on and the four of them sat down to watch a movie later that evening, Rose couldn't shake the feeling that there was something Jill and Suzie weren't telling her. Some feeling they had, or a clue they had found, which they weren't sharing. She put the thought to the back of her mind and, soon after, decided to call it a night.

That night, Suzie had already voiced her desire to wear the pyjamas, and for once, Jill didn't argue. She understood what Suzie wanted to do – she wanted to get as far as she could into the dream without being woken up – perhaps to prepare herself for the following day, perhaps just to get some closure. Either way, she agreed that neither she nor Melissa would wake Suzie – no matter what happened.

29

It was about 2am that Melissa awoke suddenly, dragging herself out from the depths of a sleep that had been fractured and
full of her own dreams. Looking over at Suzie she immediately
saw what had woken her and, remembering her promise, left
Suzie in the midst of her own dream to go and wake up Jill.

Having Jill by her side as they watched Suzie experience
the now-familiar signs of distress and terror made it easier,
and the two of them managed to move Suzie to the floor to
make sure she couldn't fall out of bed and wake herself up.

An hour or so passed, and when Suzie appeared to be
sleeping a little soundly, the two of them decided it was
time they tried to get some sleep themselves – Jill pen-
ning a short note to Suzie explaining that while Melissa
was taking her bed, Jill herself would be on the sofa. After
a moment's thought, Jill tore another piece of paper off and
left it, with a pen, on top of her note. She knew Suzie would
want to write down everything she had seen.

☉☉☉

When she opened her eyes again, it was light outside and
the sound of Rose in the kitchen and the kettle boiling filled

her ears. Stretching, she went upstairs to check on Suzie and was relieved to see her daughter sat up in bed, scrawling on the paper she had left beside her just hours before.

'Give me a minute, Mum, I'm just writing it all down,' Suzie stated before Jill could even open her mouth. 'You're not going to believe what I saw. I don't even know what to say to Sarah today!'

When Suzie finally made her way downstairs, the others were all grouped around the kitchen table waiting.

'Morning, love,' Rose stated as she put a plate of toast in front of Suzie, who eagerly snatched up a piece. She suddenly realised how hungry she was and bit into the toast while brandishing her piece of paper.

'So...' began Melissa. 'Any idea what we're up against today?'

Suzie's look became serious. 'Look, guys, I don't think we're going to find anything at the house. I mean, I still want to go... I want to see if the setup is the same as the house in my dream. But, oh god, if it is... it's so awful,' and with that she put her toast down and stared out the window where she saw a magpie.

'It's that magpie again,' she said pointing. 'I know it's trying to tell me something, I just know.'

The others just nodded, so she continued.

'I saw more after what happened last time. After Louise was in the kitchen, and she banged her head – you know, when I woke up before? But this time, I didn't wake up, but I wasn't her anymore either. I was sort of just there – and he was there too, just watching over her. Then it was like time flashed forward a little bit, and suddenly he was rolling Louise up in this rug. Then there were these woods... and a shovel, and he dug a hole...'

As she said those final words and the realisation hit all of them, Suzie began to sob.

'Awful, it was... he covered her over. I don't think I can do this today. I can't go and see him. What if it's true?'

Looking up, she saw her mum making her way over before enveloping her in a huge hug. 'Today is going to be hard, Suzie. We knew that. Let's take it one step at a time. I'll be with you, and Melissa and Grandma too, if you want them?'

Considering for a moment, Suzie sniffed and looked at her friend, reaching for her hand. 'Could you look at the local woods for me, Mel? I know it's... a crappy job, but I need to know.'

Melissa nodded with a smile. 'Of course, whatever you need.'

'It was a small wood, dense. It can't be far,' Suzie offered as Melissa nodded again.

'We're on it, Suze.'

30

They all got into the car, having decided that Jill and Suzie would drop Rose and Melissa off at the library on their way to Mr Crabtree's and arranged to meet back at the house later that day. Jill quickly reached over to Suzie giving her a quick hug. 'It'll be fine,' she said – she didn't need to say any more.

◉◉◉

Pulling up outside the library, Melissa and Rose jumped out and made their way inside – intent on doing Suzie's request justice and hopefully finding the very woods she had seen in her dream.

As they found a couple of free desks and computers, they sat down to start checking out all the woods in the local vicinity. 'You know, we could be here for a while, Rose,' pointed out Melissa as she scrolled through all the Google results of local woods to Epping. 'Epping Forest is made up of loads of pockets of woodland… it could be any one of these!'

Rose didn't say anything, just shrugged and turned back to her own research into the land ownership of Essex.

⊙⊙⊙

While this was happening, Jill and Suzie were just pulling up outside Mr. Crabtree's house. Though the day promised to be as stressful as the one before, Jill was relieved to see that Mr. Crabtree himself looked more relaxed – greeting them with a handshake. 'I think you can call me Brian now,' he added. 'Sarah's waiting for you.'

They stepped in and found Sarah shivering a little despite the warm weather outside. 'Hello,' she started timidly. 'I can't exactly say it's nice to see you again… but I appreciate you coming back.'

It was obvious that Sarah had barely slept a wink, and Jill felt an overwhelming desire to protect this woman from whatever it was they were facing.

With that, and with little else left to say, they all traipsed out to Brian's car and began their journey to Andy's – each steeling themselves for what they would find.

Jill had told Suzie not to say anything about her most recent dream, wanting to keep the grim finality of the truth away from Sarah for as long as possible – or at least until they could be more certain that it was the truth.

It was Brian who knocked on Andy's door in the end, Suzie taking a step back away from the front door – which, she was afraid to admit, held a faint glimmer of recognition.

The man who opened the door, brought to life now in stark reality, shocked her. She had known it would be him, and yet seeing him standing there, sneering at Sarah, made her want to run a mile and never look back.

Sarah, meanwhile, was standing her ground and asked, without a trace of emotion in her voice, if they could please come in.

'Why the audience, Sarah?' he asked pleasantly enough – though the smile didn't quite reach his eyes as he looked first at Jill and then at Suzie.

'This is my neighbour, Jill, and her daughter, Suzie. They're here to help,' rattled off Sarah; the lie coming easily to her. 'Dad just drove us here,' she added to explain the presence of Brian – who was glaring at Andy with a mixture of trepidation and loathing on his face.

Not taking his eyes off the group of them, Andy stood aside and widened the door a little – as much of an invitation as they were going to get.

As soon as they were through the threshold, Sarah took it upon herself to distract Andy – bustling around and wondering aloud whereabouts she had left various items she wanted to collect. Brian stood by the front door while Andy perched himself uneasily against a sideboard in the hallway – his face the picture of impatience, his foot tapping loudly on the floor.

'What do you really want, Sarah? You here for your stuff? Well, good, go and grab it and get out – it's all rubbish anyway.'

Hearing those words, Suzie was surprised that Sarah didn't lash out – particularly after what she had told her the day before. This man was bad – even she could tell that, and they'd only been in the house for a short time.

Seeing an opportunity when Andy barged into the living room to give Sarah some more grief, Suzie grabbed her mum's hand and made for the stairs, tiptoeing up them so as not to draw attention to themselves.

Suzie knew there was nothing up there that they would find, but she wanted to see if she recognised anything. Coming to the first door at the top of the landing, they opened the door to find it was Louise's bedroom.

Straight away Suzie sensed something was wrong, she wasn't sure what at first but then it hit her. To someone quickly entering the room and looking round no-one would have noticed anything was wrong, but knowing what Suzie had seen in her dream, she could sense something was missing. Taking a moment to look around, you could see the border round the carpet was lighter in shade where it looked like a rug had once been in the middle of the room. Suzie just knew that the rug used to wrap Louise in, had come from her own bedroom.

This was all happening so fast, and she knew that pretty soon she was going to be faced with the biggest question of all – what had happened to Louise?

Her mind flicked towards Melissa and her gran for a moment, and she wondered briefly if she had time to drop Mel a quick text and see how they were getting on in their hunt for the woods. But just as she was about to pull out her phone, Sarah's voice grew louder, and she realised they were coming up the stairs. Time to move.

Pulling the door closed behind her and her mum, as quietly as she could, she turned around and came face to face with Sarah. The question in Sarah's eyes was unmistakable, and Suzie could do nothing but shrug.

The bedroom she had come from – Louise's old bedroom – was the one in her dream and the rest of the house, the layout, seemed familiar. And there were details she knew she had seen before – that plant stand in the corner, and the slight curve in the stairs.

'Mum, we need to go, now,' she muttered at Jill, who nodded and put an arm around Sarah – who was now standing in the doorway of her daughter's old bedroom, clearly lost in memories. Suzie knew she was crying; but right now, she wanted nothing more than to be away from this house, so she tugged at her mum's arm again.

Jill glanced quickly at Suzie, momentarily cross at her daughter's insensitivity. But, catching the look on her face,

Jill realised things were getting a bit much for Suzie. She didn't know who to help first.

'Come on, Sarah,' said Jill gently, 'let's get some things of Louise's for you to take home, and then we can get back and think this through. I think you need a drink as well – we all do, really. We'll wait for you just downstairs, okay?'

Not waiting for an answer, Jill turned and walked with Suzie back down the stairs, rejoining Brian, who had, by now, moved into the sitting room and was casting frequent glances over at Andy.

Andy, meanwhile, looked like he didn't have a care in the world, slouched in a large armchair. 'She nearly done?' he cocked his head towards the stairs. 'Only, I need to get back to my stall.'

Suzie regarded him with distrust – she couldn't believe Sarah had lived with this man. She was such a lovely soul, so kind and warm. But this man was... Suzie didn't even have the words. He was just cold.

After a few minutes of silence – which felt endless to Suzie, they heard movement on the stairs and saw Sarah appear with a small box. A teddy was sticking out from the top, and the simplicity of the toy caused Jill's heart to swell. It was just like one Suzie used to have – and that made the gravity of this all too real.

Sarah's eyes found their way to Andy's, only this time the hardness was gone, replaced with a pleading. 'I've got the things I could find, the important things. But... please don't get rid of anything else. I know it's not worth anything, but she might want it... you know...'

Breaking off, her eyes still fixed on Andy, she waited for his response. He just shrugged, muttering that it wasn't worth anything anyway, so meant nothing to him. He'd leave it alone, for now.

Those final words caught Jill and, for the first time that day, she felt a swell of anger. How could this man take the life of a young girl? And more than that, how could he act so blasé, so nonchalant now, with Sarah in the room, acting like he had done nothing wrong? It was so... wrong. She knew then, with a strength unlike anything else she had experienced since they had arrived in Essex, that this man would not get away with his actions.

Opening the door to the sunshine outside, walking out of the house felt almost therapeutic, and both Jill and Suzie kept a little behind Brian and Sarah – unwilling to intrude on the moment the two of them were sharing, gazing into the box of Louise's belongings.

Piling back into the car, it seemed inevitable that they would all be going back to Brian's – although Suzie wasn't sure what else she could say today. She felt drained and she wanted to go home.

Sarah sat in the front passenger seat, her face frozen in a look of horror and sadness, and when they pulled up in front of the house, it took a moment before she moved. Jill gently nudged her shoulder from the back seat, willing her to make the journey from the car to the house – where they could all relax a little.

Standing on the front step, Jill opened her mouth and began saying she and Suzie would come back another day, but Sarah stopped her and looked at them both – her face filled with emotion and determination.

'I need to know what's happening. This is killing me, and my parents. I didn't tell you earlier, but my mum phoned last night. Turns out Dad had told her all about you and your visit. She's a bit – well, a lot – more open about these sort of things than me and my dad. You know, the visions and stuff.' At this, she indicated Suzie, who nodded lightly. 'She thinks it's great you're trying to help us. And, well, if it's good enough for Mum, then I'd like to hear what else you have to say. No matter how bad it is,' she added quickly.

Jill nodded. She understood completely.

'Yes, I understand. Of course. Are you okay, Suzie?' Jill turned to her daughter. Suzie felt lost. Of course she wasn't okay – but how could she say no to Sarah?

Brian went straight through to the kitchen and put the kettle on, vaguely asking who wanted tea and coffee but not really waiting for an answer. The rest of them trudged through to the living room and took a seat, not saying a word until they all heard the front door open, and a voice call out, 'Brian? Sarah?'

'My mum,' Sarah offered by way of an explanation, getting up and rushing towards the hallway. Though Jill and Suzie couldn't see what was happening, through Sarah's vague comments they gathered that her mother had just returned from her sister's house. Jill knew, with a tug at her heart, how much it must mean to Sarah to have her mother home with her again.

'Oh, Mum, I thought you were staying another week?' Sarah was asking as she led an older woman into the living room. The lady – Margaret – had a kind face, a tight perm softly framing her features. She smiled over at Jill and Suzie, and they both felt her warm presence immediately, relaxed and open.

'You must be joking, and miss all this? No love, after talking to you on the phone, I sorted out transport straight away. I knew not to mention anything to you and your father, though. You'd have just told me not to come!' with this final comment, Margaret smiled at Suzie, who smiled back.

Margaret took her coat off just as Brian came back in with their drinks. Introductions complete, Jill took a breath and turned to Suzie. 'When you're ready, love.'

Suzie looked up from the notepad Brian had given her when they arrived home – she had just finished jotting down everything that had happened so far, ending with the magpie that had been sitting on the stone wall as they pulled back up the driveway less than half an hour ago.

She didn't know what the magpie meant, but for the first time she found she didn't really mind. The magpie felt like an omen, helping her through all this, and for that she was grateful.

Looking up at the four of them waiting for her to speak, she wanted so much to tell Sarah everything, but suddenly her mouth was dry, and nothing came out. Tears welled up in her eyes, and she shook her head just a little.

Jill, noticing her daughter's distress, knew what she had to do. And with that, she started at the beginning, telling Sarah everything that Suzie – and they as a group – had gone through since they first arrived in Epping.

Though she had heard much of it before, Sarah seemed to be hanging on every word, and when Suzie finally took over to share the developments from the night before, Sarah was wide-eyed, clutching both her parents' hands in her own.

'It was so real, Sarah. Do you want me to continue?' Suzie asked uncertainly, knowing that the final bit of the story would be the hardest bit to hear.

Sarah nodded. 'I do understand how hard it is for you to tell me. It must have been awful for you… watching my daughter go through this… knowing there was nothing you could do. You're so brave, but I need you to be brave one more time and tell me, Suzie.'

Suzie nodded and carried on, her voice barely more than a whisper. 'Well, after arguing with her, he lost his temper and hit Louise across the face and told her to get out of his house. Louise fought back, and she carried on hitting him – which only seemed to make it worse. He was even more angry. They fell down the stairs, Louise getting to the bottom first, and though she tried to get up and run, he grabbed her ankle and pulled her back. From what I saw, she managed to kick him, which loosened his grip, and she made her way into the kitchen… but he wasn't far behind. He pushed her to the floor, and as she fell, she hit her head on the corner of the unit. She dropped down again, but this time she didn't get back up.

'Your ex – Andy – he just sat slouched on the floor near her for ages. He tried to find a pulse, but…'

Suzie stopped short and looked at her mum, Jill nodding to let her know she could carry on.

'I have notes here; the dates I dreamt and everything I saw,' she said, reaching for the notes in her bag. 'Do you want to… would you rather read them?'

'Tell me one thing. She's not still in the house, is she? I couldn't live knowing I was there if she…'

'No, no,' Suzie said hurriedly, shaking her head. 'I wouldn't have let you… I wouldn't have done that.'

Suzie looked at the rest of them; Margaret quietly crying, Sarah's eyes wide with shocked disbelief, Brian's face as still as stone.

Nobody had their arm around Brian – he was the one keeping them all going, but the look etched onto his face spoke of a million emotions.

Suzie carried on. 'It seemed that from the moment he realised Louise wasn't breathing, he panicked. He went out of the room and came back with a rug; I guess it was the one missing from her bedroom. He placed the rug down quite gently and rolled Louise onto it, letting it cover over her in a wrap.

'He went out to his car – checking first to see if anyone was around – then carried her out and placed her on the back seat in the rug. I guess... well, he seemed quite calm and methodical. Like he was worried about DNA or hair evidence – all the things you see on TV. He definitely did a check of the seats and the doors...'

She trailed off, the look on Sarah's face making her catch her breath.

'So,' Sarah said slowly. 'You're telling me it looked like an accident, but then he planned the detail – right down to DNA and hair evidence?'

Suzie didn't know what to say. 'I don't... I mean, I guess it was an accident, but when he realised what he'd done, he knew he had to move her without leaving evidence. Maybe that was all he could come up with.'

'Sorry, love,' Sarah shook her head. 'I'm not trying to question you. I'm trying to understand – to get into his head. To work out who would do such a thing to someone they knew...'

'If you want me to stop, I will.'

'No, no, I need to know now, and then we can call the police.' The last remark was made pointedly to Brian, who nodded curtly.

'I just don't think they'll believe me,' Suzie said, voicing the concern that had been at the back of her mind ever since they first came across Sarah and her family.

'But they will have to if I back you up. I want them to know who did it. Have you got more to tell me, Suzie? Do you know where she is? Because the police told me they had searched our house and found nothing, but if you have any ideas at all...'

'There was nothing to find, I don't think. I didn't see any... blood, if that's what you mean.'

Sarah shook her head again and put her hands over her mouth – clearly filling her mind with the ways in which her daughter had died. It was an awful sight to behold.

'Look, please, I want to stop,' said Suzie desperately. 'You're upset, and I don't want to upset you anymore.'

Suzie was now also sobbing, clutching at her mum. It felt like she had lost someone too.

At this, Sarah seemed to regain a little strength. 'They did say they found a lot of fingerprints of Louise's in the kitchen, but to be honest I never thought anything of it. They didn't either, especially when I explained that we had a dog, and she was often the one who fed it, rolling around on the floor play fighting and cuddling him.'

'Where is the dog now?' said Suzie, realising with a start that she had never seen a dog in her dreams – nor any sign of one in the houses they had visited.

'It was an old dog,' answered Sarah with a sad smile. 'Died around two months before Louise went missing. Poor Louise was distraught. She had been brought up with Pebbles. Have you got any pets, Suzie?' she added.

'No, I used to. A dog called Trixie. I can understand how upset Louise felt. I was the same.'

'So, where do we go from here?' said Margaret, returning to the story. Jill could see it took all her strength to speak, and she felt a warm rush of affection for the older woman. Just like her own mother – always keeping them on track. 'After you saw Andrew putting my granddaughter in his car, what happened then?'

And so, with a newfound strength, Suzie carried on – spurred on by the magpie which now sat, just out of her line of sight, on the windowsill.

'After he put Louise in his car, he drove to some woods. We're trying to work out where, my friend and my gran... they're at the library, looking. He carried her out of his car – he had a spade – and he walked with Louise over his shoulder. He must have been quite strong. He didn't seem like he was struggling, and he walked for ages. He seemed to hesitate at one point, and he looked around him. He had a torch on his phone – it was quite dark by then – and then he dropped everything in this one area and started digging.'

Suzie looked over at the patio window, and this time she saw the magpie, sitting as still as a statue, looking directly at her. She felt comforted and spurred on to finish.

But before she could continue, Brian finally spoke – the sound of his voice reverberating around the room. 'I think I should hear the rest. Sarah, you've heard enough. This is up to me now.'

Surprisingly, they all agreed, and with a little relief, Jill led Sarah and Margaret outside, leaving Suzie and Brian in the living room.

By this point, Suzie felt completely drained; lost in what had happened over the past week. Brian, possibly realising she needed a minute, disappeared to make more drinks – bringing a steaming cup of coffee back to Suzie and handing it to her with a smile.

'It's nearly over, Suzie. Tell me the rest, and I'll work out what we need to do.' And despite everything, Suzie felt a wave of gratitude wash over her, with someone else promising to take over. She just had to tell the last little bit.

'After he dug the hole, he picked Louise up, still in the rug, and placed her in the hole. It was quite deep, I remember that, and he was quite gentle. He didn't drop her. Then he started covering her up,' Suzie was talking slowly and quietly.

'After he covered Louise up, he just looked around again and pulled some undergrowth over the area. Then, he just casually walked back to his car, putting the spade back in the boot.

I was kind of there with him, like in the earlier dreams. I was Louise, but at this point I was just there – not me but someone else. And then he drove home. That was when I woke up.'

Brian just sat there for a moment, taking it all in. It wasn't lost on him that this could well be the moment that ended six months of wondering and pain. Six months not knowing where Louise was. Could she really be somewhere close – buried in the ground beneath a pile of undergrowth and dirt?

31

'Right then,' Brian said sharply after a moment, standing up so suddenly that Suzie almost jumped.

'There's only one thing to do now, and we're going to need your help, Suzie.'

She nodded slowly. 'I know what you're going to say. Mum and I have already talked about it. It's time to go to the police.'

Brian gave a sharp nod. 'We have more than enough evidence now, don't you think? The way he treats my daughter, for one...' he tailed off, shaking his head slightly.

Suzie didn't want to ask, but she knew she had to.

'Shouldn't we find Louise first? As I mentioned, my friend, Melissa, and my grandma... they're at the library now, looking at the different woods in the area. Trying to work out where he might have taken her. I mean, let's face it. He can't have gone too far.'

Brian slowly sat back in his chair, the cogs of his mind whirring. As much as he wanted to take action against Andy now, he knew Suzie was right. Until there was a body, there was no crime.

It pained him to think of Louise as a body, and for a moment his head span with the gravity of what he had just thought. Louise was still alive in his mind, and he didn't want to give up on that – not for a second. But at the same time...

'Yes, you're right. We need to keep looking. You say your friend and your grandmother are already on the case, looking for the woods?'

'Yes, and Brian, we won't stop until he is behind bars, but I think... me and Mum should go home now. You all need space. Perhaps we could see you tomorrow to flesh things out and decide what to do?' she asked questioningly, unsure if what she was suggesting was the right thing to do.

'Yes,' Brian agreed. 'I think we all need a little time to... process this development. Before we jump right into whatever happens next.'

He didn't need to say anything more.

'What do you think the police will say?' asked Suzie, voicing a question that had been at the back of her mind for a while.

'I don't know,' he said thoughtfully. 'I can tell you one thing, though, I won't be leaving the station until I know they are doing something about it. Yes, it's farfetched, and yes, I initially thought you were insane. But now... we need to find Louise so we can make him pay.'

'You mean... find her ourselves? Actually, FIND her?' Suzie asked, unable to hide her horror.

Brian just nodded. 'I'll be damned if I have to sit back and wait another minute for those cops to do something. You've done more in the last few days than they have in six months, and I won't let it end now.'

Suzie paused, unsure what to say. She hated the idea of having to do this themselves, and yet...

Brian broke her train of thought suddenly, his words cutting through the silence that had fallen after his rant. You should head off home now, let everyone have some space. I must say to you, thank you for persevering. It took a lot for

you to come back and say all that, and...' his voice cracked
a little, the anger melting away.

Suzie just nodded, and the two of them headed outside
to meet up with Jill and finally make their way home.

32

When they walked into the empty house – Melissa and Rose were still out – Jill audibly sighed, the sound filling the hallway. 'Maybe they couldn't find the woods if they're still not back yet,' she wondered aloud.

Suzie nodded and went straight to the kitchen, suddenly famished and looking for a snack.

Not ten minutes later, the door opened again, and Melissa and Rose rushed in, full of questions and updates.

Nodding at Jill, who was already making sandwiches and had offered one to the two of them, Melissa launched right into it. 'What did they say?' she asked breathlessly, Rose hanging on her every word.

'They were distraught, as you can imagine,' began Suzie. 'We told them everything, even about you looking for the woods today.'

'She did really well. Sarah, that is,' added Jill. 'Although she couldn't listen to everything. Suzie had to tell Brian, the grandfather, the last bit on his own.' At this, she glanced proudly at Suzie.

'So, did you find anything at the library?' asked Suzie, turning back to her friend. 'Are there many woods or forests we need to be looking at?'

'Well, the good news is that there are only two woods to consider,' started Melissa. 'The bad news is that one of them is sixty-five acres, so you can imagine how long that would take to look through… I honestly think the police would refuse to even begin a search there, what with the limited information they have. The other wood is small enough though, so we could start with that,' she added brightly.

'Is that the Spensally Wood? It's only a few miles away,' commented Jill, recalling the wood and its maze-like paths from visits as a child.

'Yes,' said Melissa, nodding. 'I do think that would be the one he would have taken her to, purely based on the time period he had in which to… you know… St Mary's Wood is another five miles away, anyway, and though it doesn't sound far, given its size as well as the distance… well, that's my feeling on it anyway,' she said, tailing off.

'I think you're right, Melissa,' said Suzie, squeezing her friend's hand.

'What do Louise's family want to do? Did they believe you?' asked Rose, looking directly at Suzie.

'They did,' answered Suzie, honestly. 'At first, they didn't want to believe it, but the more detail we gave them, the more they realised that I wasn't making it up. I could tell them things about the house, the garden, even the relationship between Louise and the man… then they believed me. And when we visited the house and saw him… it was creepy,' she finished, shuddering at the memory of how vivid everything had seemed in real life after her dream.

'Didn't he remember you from when we saw him at the newsstand the other day? And when you were walking around the house, did it feel like you were, you know, alone? Or, like, was there someone with you?' asked Melissa curiously.

'Oh no,' smiled Suzie, knowing that Melissa's mind was back on those spiritual websites she had been trawling through days before. 'Nothing like that. It was just weird seeing the place in real life. As far as him remembering me, I knew he wouldn't and so in that respect I wasn't frightened at all. Let's face it, he serves that many people on a daily basis, there was no way he would have remembered me'

'I don't think you will ever hear voices,' chipped in Rose. 'It doesn't work like that. Martha never heard people… she simply had visions.'

'You know what, that's probably a good thing,' said Melissa reassuringly. 'I wouldn't want to hear voices. I wouldn't know what to do!'

'Right then,' said Jill, standing up to clear away the sandwich plates. 'We need to find out how to get to these woods and work out some sort of path through them. Do you think it's best we go on our own, or do you think we should speak to Louise's family? I think they might want to go with us,' she added, mainly to Suzie.

'Well, for a start, we already have the location of the woods and the verified footpaths. Here,' Melissa said, handing round a sheet of paper she had printed earlier that day.

Suzie took the directions of the nearest wood first, which she could now see was a maze of footpaths – though the site seemed small.

'Well,' she began. 'From looking at this, if we go on our own tomorrow morning Mum, you said it would only take us about fifteen to twenty minutes to get there?'

'What if Louise's family want to go with us, we need to give them that option?' said Jill again, conscious that Louise's relatives were expecting to hear from them tomorrow morning at the latest.

'Yes, I know. I just want to give them a rest tonight. I agree with Mel. Just from looking at the other forest, it would have taken him a bit longer, and it's so huge… it doesn't add up.'

'In your dream, Suzie, did you have any idea of timescales or timings...' asked Jill hopefully.

'I wish,' smiled Suzie. 'I just know it was dark. If we think about the time she left home, everything that happened... it probably would have been after midnight. But after that, I have no idea.'

After a few hours of television and a round of hot chocolates, they all decided to get to bed early – unsure what the following day would bring but sure that whatever it was, they would need to be well rested.

Further discussion had led them to decide to call Brian first thing and tell him the whole plan. They will leave it then with Brian to talk through with Sarah. If they wanted to join them at the smaller woods, they should have that option.

As she pulled on her own silky short pyjamas, Suzie folded Louise's old pyjamas up carefully and placed them on a chair. It seemed strange that somehow, she had become connected to this girl through their shared ownership of a pair of pyjamas. If you had asked Suzie how it worked, she couldn't have told you – and really, she thought, she didn't think it mattered much how it happened. The fact was, she could see what happened, and that had helped them get this far. Maybe tomorrow, they could finally find out the whole truth and get some justice for Louise.

33

The following morning dawned bright and sunny, and as Jill got out of bed, she felt a sense of trepidation run through her body, combined with an intense nervous energy.

The first thing she wanted to do was call Brian and explain what their plans were, and to see if they wanted to join them at the woods. She had no doubt they would and was fully expecting to see him them all there when they arrived – if not with Margaret in tow as well.

Sarah was the first to answer the phone, listening quietly before passing the phone to Brian. It seemed Sarah wasn't ready to confront what was happening. Brian did not hesitate before accepting the invitation, however, and said he would pick them up on his way past.

They decided that Rose, too, would stay home, as not only was she feeling emotionally exhausted, but she no longer felt she had the strength to help anyone else – never mind herself. She had wept for Louise the night before, and for her own grandmother, Martha, and knew she would only get in the way today.

Brian arrived at their home half an hour later, looking like he hadn't slept all night. Something which was soon confirmed by the large flask of coffee in the drinks holder.

Without speaking, Brian, Jill, Suzie and Melissa got into the car and, after a cursory glance at the directions, began on their way. It only took around twenty minutes to arrive at the woods, but it was the longest twenty minutes they had all experienced; the silence in the car was interrupted only by the occasional car horn and the distinct tinkle of the morning ice cream van making the rounds.

Brian parked up, stopping to let a few walkers cross the entrance and make their way into the woods. Aside from them, there were only a few cars parked up, mostly made up of locals out to walk their dogs or joggers seeking a different route.

'Do you know where you're going?' asked Brian – the first words any of them had uttered since they began their journey.

'Not really,' admitted Suzie, who, beyond arriving at the woods, hadn't given their next steps much thought at all. She wasn't even sure which direction they should be heading in.

Just as she glanced around widely, something caught her eye, and her gaze landed abruptly on a magpie perched on a nearby fence just to the right of the park's entranceway.

'Could it be...?' she whispered aloud, before nudging her mum and pointing.

'I think it's this way,' she said a little louder, addressing the whole group now, before walking slowly towards the bird. As she reached it, the bird took off and swooped low, covering ground faster than they could on foot but still remaining within their line of sight.

As they progressed into the woods, the trees became more densely packed and the canopy thicker, creating a darker environment. Once or twice Suzie thought she had lost sight of the bird, only to be brought back on track by a waft of its wings or a quiet call.

And then it stopped, perched on a dead log just fifty yards or so in front of the group.

As they approached, Suzie not taking her eyes off the log where the magpie landed, the bird rose up and landed on a branch above them, hovering gently. Suzie knew now, looking about her, that this was it.

'Is this it?' Brian asked, breaking the silence and echoing the very same thoughts that were running through everyone's minds. Suzie aware of the significance of the magpie, quickly nodded, adding quietly, 'I think so.'

An air of reverence hung around the group as they considered what to do next. None of them had really considered how finding the site would make them feel, but as they stood and stared about them, a wave of raw emotion washed over them.

Suzie stepped forward and waved her arm over a hedgerow. 'I think it was here,' she said, beckoning Brian forward and helping him drag some of the greenery away, clearing an area.

After a few moments, Melissa stepped forward to help, and soon the whole group of them were tugging at undergrowth and branches, trying their best to reach the ground at the bottom and clear enough space. They didn't talk, but they worked in companionable enough silence; each motivated by the thought of finally putting the mystery to bed and being able to put a guilty man behind bars.

As she had so many times in the previous days, Suzie thought back to Martha's diaries and wondered if this was how she had felt when she neared the resolution of her first mystery. Suzie hadn't known what to expect, but for some reason, she hadn't anticipated such an ominous weight on her shoulders. Looking up, she noticed the magpie had gone and suddenly felt overwhelmed with sadness.

After about fifteen minutes, they finally had a clear access to a space of ground. The soil looked no different, though enough time had passed for this not to be too unexpected. It definitely didn't look like it was concealing a body.

Again, it was Brian who voiced what they were all thinking. 'Are you sure?' he asked. 'It doesn't look like the kind of spot…'

Suzie shook her head, then replied simply, 'I'm 100%.'

'Well, I suppose that's got us this far,' Brian said, shrugging. 'If you're right, we probably need more than a few garden spades. I think it's time to see the police.'

'I can't see them turning us away,' added Melissa. 'Not with all this evidence. Surely, they would at least have to look into it, visit the site…'

They all nodded.

'That's it then,' said Jill decidedly. 'Let's go. But before we do, how are we going to mark this spot?'

'We leave signs,' said Melissa after a minute. 'Mark the path with twigs, leaves, whatever we can find.'

It was certainly the best – and the only idea they had, so the group set about sourcing piles of broken twigs, odd logs and a handful of rocks. Once they were certain they had enough to mark their trail, they made their way slowly back to the car, using their gatherings to mark the path they took.

Once back at the car, Suzie took one last long look into the woods before turning away and getting into the car with the others. She couldn't be sure, but she felt, deep inside her, as if this was the last moment of uncertain peace that Louise would have, here in the depths of the wood.

Pulling up outside the Police Station, they quickly ascertained that no one wanted to be left behind, so they all made their way in. Suzie took her notes, knowing that she couldn't possibly leave a single detail out, while Jill clutched a bag holding the pyjamas. She knew it was a long shot but having them might just be helpful.

Brian did the talking at first, asking to speak to somebody in charge of Louise's case. After a few moments of searching on a database, the receptionist told them to sit tight and wait for the Superintendent.

'I'd better call your grandma,' Jill muttered to Suzie, who nodded tightly and continued staring at the station doors. It took a further eighteen minutes for the Superintendent to arrive – every one of them counted minutely and meticulously by the ticking of the clock on the wall opposite them.

It felt like a lifetime.

'Come with me please,' the Superintendent finally called, waving them towards him just as Jill reappeared.

Following him through a large set of heavy doors, Jill couldn't help thinking of her favourite police dramas, where the station always felt like a sanctuary of safety and re-assurance, and doughnut-eating policemen. In the flesh, though, the white-washed walls and echoing corridors were intimidating.

'Right,' the man said as they filed into a cramped meeting room. 'To introduce myself, I'm Superintendent Carpenter and I can do this with you all together, or we can talk individually. It's up to you. As far as I'm aware, you're here to volunteer information, is that right?' He gestured with his hand for them to sit down. Albeit only two chairs available for visitors, Suzie made reference to both Jill and Brian take them.

'Yes,' Jill began before Brian took over.

'You need to listen to the girl,' he said, indicating Suzie. 'And we'll all stay,' he added firmly.

Just then a policewoman walked in, and they were each introduced to PC Kelly Jenkins.

'Don't worry about Kelly,' the Superintendent said. 'She's just here as a witness to what you have to say.' He turned to Suzie. 'In your own time,' he added kindly.

And so, it began, from the beginning, all over again.

Suzie started with their arrival in Essex, the piles of clothes and the strange pyjamas buried in with the tops and skirts. The dreams and the nightmares, explaining how it wasn't until she saw the man from her dreams working outside the Oxford Street tube station that she started taking it seriously.

Occasionally Jill chipped in, describing the violence of the dreams and how Suzie's body responded to what her unconscious mind was seeing.

Suzie carried on talking until she had told them everything, secretly relieved and a little surprised that they had let her speak uninterrupted, with not so much as a smirk or a raised eyebrow.

Finally, she finished, sitting back and taking a long gulp of water. PC Jenkins smiled at her.

'Right, Suzie, so the house you visited was the same as in the dream, correct? And the woods? And did you find anything there?'

'We think we found the spot,' answered Suzie. 'We didn't dig anything, though – we came straight here.'

PC Jenkins nodded, whilst the Superintendent straightened up, taking it all in.

'I'll be honest. Under different circumstances I wouldn't give you the time of day with this. It's… it's unlike anything I've heard before.'

At this, Suzie took a huge breath, feeling her chest wobble a little.

He paused before continuing, 'And that's what makes me so certain that what you're saying is true. Whether it leads to anything is another matter, and something we will look into immediately, but the fact that you – all of you – believe it to be true gives me reason to believe you.'

He turned to Brian. 'Mr. Crabtree, you know how much time we have given your granddaughter's case, and I cannot blame you for bringing this to our attention. Given the links, the vivid visions and the backed research you have brought today, I suggest you all head home and let me speak with my superiors. But we will call you, and we will need you to attend the site with us – at least one or two of you.'

They all nodded, unsure whether or not to believe what he was saying. They had each expected to be laughed out of the station door, perhaps even arrested for wasting time. But as they walked out towards the door, they could clearly hear, some way behind them, the Superintendent dialing the phone and asking to speak to the Chief.

◉◉◉

'... I know it's hard to believe, Sir, it took me a while too. But I think we should go ahead. It's better than no leads.'

'You're telling me that you believe in ghost stories and witches and hippy magic?'

'No, Sir. With all due respect, you didn't see them. They don't want anything. They don't even want to be a part of this, Sir. You can see it in their faces. The grandfather, he was here too, and he said even the mum believes it.'

'I can't believe I'm saying this, but you have a good instinct Carpenter and so I'll give it a chance. But you report back to me immediately, and if this is the work of time wasters, then I want them brought back to the station. When can you do it?'

'Tomorrow, Sir. I'll call in support and get three PCs to the scene.'

'I'll expect your report by 6pm tomorrow.'

'Very good, Sir... Thank you.'

◉◉◉

Later that evening, Jill received a call from Brian confirming the full search, commencing at 9.30am the following morning.

He requested the presence of Suzie, who readily agreed. She was ready.

34

As she climbed into bed that night, it was all Suzie could do to keep her eyes away from the pyjamas. She couldn't believe it was nearly over, though a part of her was relieved she would never again have to see the visions of Louise.

The next morning, after forcing down a piece of toast which she really didn't feel like, Suzie found herself being escorted out to a police car by a young woman in uniform, waving to her family who stood on the front doorstep, watching her go.

Quickly walking up to Suzie and giving her one final hug, Jill whispered in Suzie's ear, 'I'm so proud of you. We'll be right here waiting when you get back.' Suzie just nodded, then turned and gave Melissa a hug who had followed Jill to the police car.

Melissa had been a great friend through all this, and Suzie couldn't think how she had gotten so lucky. With no thought of her own summer plans, Melissa had cancelled going back home just to stay with Suzie; supporting her through late-night talks, walks and glasses of wine under the setting sun. This time together was just what Suzie had needed, and she decided, there and then, that when this was all over, she would treat Melissa to a weekend away. Somewhere all this, the visions and the pyjamas wouldn't follow them.

Brian was already in the vehicle when Suzie climbed in, giving him a small smile and a nod. She suddenly found that she was no longer nervous as she sat in companionable silence with the man she had come to respect and know as Louise's grandfather. She wasn't exactly happy about any of this, but she finally felt content – like they were doing something good.

Of course, all of this was tinged with an undercurrent question that she couldn't shake off.

Why her?

Over the last week or so, she had thought about that one question more and more. Perhaps her great-gran was watching over her and knew that Suzie could cope, or maybe it was just pure coincidence. If it was her great-gran's doing, Suzie didn't know whether she should be thanking or cursing her. After all, yes, she was helping people, but when it really came down to it, the ability to see the visions and actions of others was an unnatural phenomenon that she didn't feel able to handle.

Glancing out the window, she realised that suddenly they weren't far away from the woods at all, and her belly gave a quick flutter of nerves.

When they arrived, there were at least four other police vehicles waiting there, as well as a police van and a cluster of individuals – some in full white suits. As she stepped out of the car, Suzie also noticed a police dog, poised and ready at the edge of the path.

'That's to sniff the area where we think Louise might be,' the police officer said, nodding towards the large Alsatian. Brian nodded his approval. They seemed to be taking this seriously, and for that, both he and Suzie were grateful.

'Right, Suzie,' said Superintendent Carpenter, striding over to them.

As he approached, Suzie suddenly felt a little sick. What if there was nothing to be found, and she had brought them all here for no reason? All she had were visions and dreams. Suddenly, the whole charade felt so absurd that she wanted to cry and blurt out apologies to the police, to Brian, to Louise's family...

Almost as if reading her mind, Superintendent Carpenter's face relaxed into a smile.

'Don't worry about anything. If we don't find anything where you said, it will only be good news. After all, if you are wrong about the position, it could be that Louise is still alive and well.'

Suzie nodded, and Brian put his hand on her arm. He wished his wife and daughter were here, but he knew it would be too much for them.

'Which way, Suzie?' asked Carpenter, beckoning over another officer who looked to be the leader of the team awaiting instruction.

'This way,' Suzie pointed left to the woods, at a small opening through which they had all proceeded just twenty-four hours earlier.

Superintendent Carpenter led the party walking into the woods, shortly followed by Suzie and Brian, then the rest of the team. As they made their way further into the woods, the police force team fanned out, covering more ground in a move that seemed to emanate expertise and professionalism. Suzie found herself wondering how often they had to do this, and how many bodies were thoughtlessly dumped in woodlands just like these.

Looking around her, she could almost picture the full route, her pace picking up as she recognised the marks she and the others had left the day before. But it wasn't just the markings she saw. Though she would never have admitted it to anyone else around her at that moment, when she looked up, she saw her little friend, the magpie, sitting watching them. They were on the right track.

When the magpie finally flew up, arced above some trees and landed on an old log, Suzie knew they had made it.

She pointed. 'There,' she said. Her one word was enough.

Coming to a stop, Carpenter organised the police, unleashing the police dog to search the area.

Stepping out from the group, Suzie noticed for the first time that three of the officers were, in fact, labourers, not in uniform, carrying shovels. She realised with a start that they were here to dig the hole for the police.

Over the next few minutes, the police dog, a beautiful Alsatian who went by the name Belle, sniffed normally, covering the area quickly. When she suddenly went wild, Suzie wasn't sure what was happening. Had something gone wrong? Then the truth hit her with a sledgehammer.

Carpenter led Suzie and Brian away from the area as the men with shovels stepped forward and began to dig.

They only moved a few feet away, but it was enough to prevent them from seeing in the hole, and Carpenter seemed intent on distracting them further to avoid them wandering over to see what was happening.

'Do you know what the dog's digging means?' Carpenter asked them both gently.

'I do,' said Brian shortly. 'That means… you're trying to tell us that there is a body there, and it could be Louise.'

'Yes, I'm afraid so,' Carpenter nodded sadly. 'We'll know more shortly.' They were only there for about fifteen or maybe twenty minutes when one of the police officers called over to Carpenter and beckoned him over. Making his apologies, Carpenter told Suzie and Brian to stay where they were.

Carpenter went over to the officer, who offered the words, 'We've found something, sir,' before indicating the hole.

There was no mistaking what was there. A body wrapped in a rug, just like the one Suzie had described, with its intricate patterning and mud-stained colours. It was impossible to tell at the moment if it was Louise –they would have to wait for a pathologist to confirm that – but all the signs were there.

'I'll go and break the news to Brian,' Carpenter muttered quietly, walking off in the direction of Suzie and Brian.

They instantly knew it was Louise. Even though Carpenter explained that there was no way to be sure until later, Brian and Suzie both knew. When Brian made towards the hole to see for himself, Carpenter held him back.

'I don't recommend you look. Wait until we have the body removed and the pathology report.'

But Brian just shook his head. 'No. Sorry, but no, I can't just stand here knowing it's my granddaughter over there.'

'We don't know that it is Louise yet,' said Carpenter firmly, but Brian shook him off and stormed towards the hole before anyone else could stop him.

Closely following, Suzie saw Brian collapse at the side of the hole ahead of her, falling to his knees as he reached down and touched the rug. 'This is the rug from Sarah's house, I know because we bought it for Louise when they moved in with Andy for her bedroom.' he said quietly.

Carpenter rested a hand on his shoulder.

'Please go back to the car. I'll take you home.'

Brian got up slowly, and the three of them went back to the car, the journey back through the woods taking barely any time at all – the three of them lost in their own thoughts.

The trip back home was unbearable, Suzie crying silently while Brian – white as a sheet – comforted her. If anything felt like a dream, this was it. Suzie couldn't believe it had all been true.

'What happens now?' Brian asked Carpenter as they turned towards Rose's house.

'Well, we will need to do a post-mortem and then wait for their report. As long as there is enough evidence to support your story about what happened, then it looks like we can charge your daughter's ex-boyfriend.'

'I understand, but can I ask… will this be a quick matter, or will it now drag on? I don't think we can cope…'

Carpenter interrupted him before he could finish. 'It will only take a few days for the report from the post-mortem. I assure you that we will push this through to ensure we get the report as soon as possible. It will, as you can imagine, take us some time to put it all together. We need the evidence.'

Brian just nodded, no words left to say.

☉☉☉

As they arrived at Rose's home, the front door opened to reveal Suzie's family waiting. Brian asked if she wanted him there with her when she told them.

'No, it's okay. You need to get home to Sarah and your wife. I will ring you though, after the post-mortem report comes through, if that's okay?'

'We'll be there,' Brian said, smiling. 'Without you, none of this would have happened, and we'd still be looking for Louise. Me, my daughter and my wife… we can't thank you enough.'

Getting out of the vehicle, Suzie walked up the path to her grandma's front door, wishing – not for the first time – that she had just gone abroad with her friends like everyone else this summer.

As she stepped over the threshold, they were there – all of them – ready with hugs and tea and questions.

'Don't fuss, please,' Suzie said, backing away slightly. 'I'm sorry, I don't mean to be funny. I just... need my own space. I'll tell you what happened, but please, don't fuss.'

'It was so much worse than I thought. To be honest with you, I didn't think we would be there when they found Louise. I had it in my head that they would just go to the spot, let me show them where I thought it was, and then bring us home. But they just moved us along a little, out of sight of the hole, and within about half an hour or so, they had found Louise.'

Rose began to cry as Jill went white and sat still as a statue. It was Melissa who moved to comfort Suzie first, careful not to fuss or upset her further.

'So, they actually found her then,' whispered Rose; not a question, but more of a statement of disbelief.

'Yes, I didn't see her, though. Carpenter asked us to go back to the police car, but Brian looked anyway, and he went to where they had been digging... he just collapsed at the side of the hole and cried. I think I was more upset at seeing Brian cry really, to see a grown man cry... it broke me. I felt – I feel – so guilty for what I started, except he said he would always be eternally grateful for what I had done, so now I'm so confused, and I'm not sure how I feel.'

She finished her story, exhausted and emotionally drained, but glad she wasn't alone in knowing the truth anymore.

◉◉◉

The day after Suzie's encounter in the woods, the family decided to take a break and get out of the house, heading towards Southend-on-Sea for a much-needed day out. The weather was still hot, and though Suzie was still a little subdued, Jill knew that a day away from Epping was just what she needed.

The first thing they did when they parked up on the seafront was to head to the arcades, only stopping when they became hungry enough to get ice cream on the beach. They played crazy golf, Melissa, Jill and Suzie playing while Rose watched on, then went for fish and chips. At around 7pm, when they were all ready to leave for home – tanned and happier than they had felt in days, Suzie allowed herself to relax. She was shattered, and Louise was still on her mind almost constantly, but no matter what happened, they should have some answers tomorrow if not the day after.

☉☉☉

The following morning when she arrived downstairs for breakfast, Jill announced to Suzie that they would be spending the day together – starting with breakfast out. Jill had got up extra early and collected fresh pastries for Rose and Melissa, having already asked them if they would mind if she and Suzie went out for a few hours to discuss everything that had happened. She wanted to make sure Suzie was okay – really okay – and thought it would be best if she spoke with her alone for a bit.

Leaving Melissa and Rose to a morning spread of fresh pastries, coffee and lounging in the garden, Suzie and Jill headed out – borrowing Rose's car to drive into town, stopping outside a little deli called "Cucina's" which had cute umbrellas out front and a sign waving in the summer breeze.

Before they had even stepped foot in the door, Suzie's nose was full of the smells of fresh bread and cheeses and roasted coffee, and she found her mouth was already watering; her stomach far hungrier than it had felt in days if she was honest with herself.

Sitting at a small table under the edge of the deli's awning, Jill headed inside to order their coffees and pastries, adding on a small pack of different cheeses to take home for Rose and Melissa. Jill had known that the two of them would be okay with her taking Suzie out, but she still felt bad for taking Melissa's friend away from her. It felt somehow like she was rubbing her close relationship with Suzie in Melissa's face, sure that Melissa's mother would not, and did not, go to the same lengths to spend time with her daughter. Thinking again, she added an extra couple of muffins to her takeaway as well – a treat for the girls to enjoy later that night.

Having received their coffee and delicious baked goods, the two of them settled into the morning, simply enjoying each other's company, catching up on their thoughts and feelings, and reliving some of their happiest memories.

Once the sun was high enough in the sky that they thought they might melt if they stayed sat at the table any longer, Jill suggested they take a walk around the town, wanting to enjoy her daughter's company for a little longer before it was time to head back home.

Passing the charity shop where Rose had picked out the bags of clothes, and where, really, all this had begun, Suzie gestured to the door. Shrugging, Jill nodded, and they stepped inside.

As they looked around, pointing out bargains and throwing random outfits together, a lady walked right up to Suzie, hovering by her side until Suzie turned and looked her right in the eye. She was around the same height as Suzie, with dark hair and a kind face. Before Suzie could say a word, the woman spoke – five words that hit Suzie like a sledgehammer.

'Did you like the pyjamas?'

Shocked, she couldn't answer – instead, she just stared at the old lady before gazing wildly around, looking for her mum. Jill, who assumed Suzie was caught up looking at the accessory stand, had headed for the changing room to try on a dress that caught her fancy and had missed the entire exchange.

After another minute or so, the lady asked again. 'Did you like the pyjamas?'

Stumbling over her words, backing away until she was flat up against a rack of tops and skirts, Suzie's voice shook. 'How... how do you know? My grandma was here... they said there wasn't anyone here who looked...' she didn't finish her sentence because it didn't make any sense. The woman she was looking at right now, the one who had spoken, matched the description her gran had given her all those days ago. About 5'4", slim, dark hair...

'It's you...' she whispered. 'But you don't work here. You don't even... exist.'

The lady nodded gravely before her face lit up again. 'I used to work here. I used to help my goddaughter find clothes to wear to parties, things she could stitch together and turn into something beautiful.'

'Louise,' Suzie whispered again, unsure why she was whispering, but not able to raise her voice any louder.

The lady held out her hand. 'Annie, Annie Fuller. I understand you have found Louise and discovered what happened. I'm glad about that,' she added, smiling sadly. And then, before she could move away or say another word, Suzie felt a cold movement brush against her cheek as Annie touched her face ever so gently. And then she was gone.

Seeing her mum emerging from the changing room, Suzie hurried over to her. 'Mum, did you see that woman? The one who was speaking to me?'

As her mum shook her head, Suzie turned sharply towards the shop assistant. 'Did you?' Another shake, another no.

Suzie was lost in thought, certain that what she had just seen was 100% real, and yet…

'There's only Maxine and me in today, love,' added the shop assistant. 'What did she look like?'

Suzie described Annie, careful to make sure she didn't miss anything out. But the shop assistant still looked lost and just shook her head again.

'Can you get Maxine out here, please, so that I can tell if it was her or not?' Suzie asked, aware that she was clutching at straws but unsure what other explanation there could be.

'Maxine?' called the shop assistant. 'Can you just come out here a minute? Somebody wants to see you.' But as soon as Maxine appeared, Suzie knew she was wasting their time. Maxine was younger than Annie had been, and a few inches taller. 'Thanks anyway,' she muttered as Jill paid for her dress, and the two of them turned to leave the shop.

As they stepped into the street, Jill turned straight to Suzie and looked her in the eye. 'What's wrong, love? What just happened?'

Suzie was pale, her eyes a little haunted. 'I think I saw the lady Grandma described, who sold her the pyjamas. Her name was Annie, and she was Louise's godmother… she kissed my cheek, and she was so cold.'

Shivering slightly at the memory, she put her cardigan on she'd been carrying with her and dug her hands into her pockets, drawing it closer around her. As she did, her hands brushed against something small and delicate in the pocket – something which she hadn't put there herself. Pulling it out, she opened her hand to reveal a small silver bracelet.

'This isn't mine...' she said slowly.

Jill laughed. 'It must be. You just forgot about it, what with all your lovely things!'

'No, honestly Mum, it's not. There wasn't anything in my pockets when we left.' Suzie didn't know what was going on, but she suddenly felt so overwhelmed.

'Come on, sweetheart, let's head back home and see the others.'

◎◎◎

When they arrived home, Rose was on the phone. 'Oh, hang on a minute, Brian. Suzie's just walked in,' she said down the phone, handing Suzie the handset.

'Hi, Brian. Yes... oh okay... At the station? Yes, no, that's no problem. I've just got in, it's fine. See you in half an hour then. Bye, Brian.' And she hung up, Jill watching her with her eyebrows slightly raised.

'They've done the post-mortem,' Suzie said, in answer to the question that her mum didn't even need to ask. 'Superintendent Carpenter wants to see me and Brian at the station. Mum, will you...'

Jill nodded. 'I'll come with you, love.'

Rose bustled back into the hallway with a tray of home-made lemonade. 'You've still got half an hour, did you say? Well then, let's have a drink and enjoy this glorious sunshine. I tell you, Melissa has been working awfully hard with me in the garden this morning. She's a real gem,' she added, smiling as they headed out the back door into the garden, where Melissa was hunched over the vegetable patch.

'Is Brian going on his own?' Jill asked as they sat down.

'No, Sarah's going as well. She needs to go, I guess they'll say things about Louise that Sarah will need to hear,' Suzie said thoughtfully, secretly thinking she couldn't think of anything worse than hearing what had happened to Louise, with Louise's mum right next to her.

Twenty-five minutes later, they heard Brian pulling up onto the drive – bang on time, as always.

'Nearly over,' whispered Rose, squeezing Suzie's arm as she and Jill got up to leave. Melissa, turning to see her friend about to leave, ran over and gave her a massive hug. She didn't need to say anything.

They drew apart as they heard the car door shut, and with a final smile at her gran, Suzie and Jill turned and walked out to meet Brian.

As they approached the car, Jill noticed that Sarah had her head down, tears visible on her cheeks. Jill could only imagine what she was going through and found herself reaching across and squeezing Suzie's hand suddenly and desperately. Like Sarah, Jill had only one child, and a life without her was unthinkable.

They arrived at the Police Station some twenty minutes later where Superintentdent Carpenter was waiting for them in the main reception area of the station. As soon as he saw them, he rushed over, beckoning them through, down the corridor and into his office.

A young officer arrived with a tray of tea and biscuits, and the four of them seated themselves in front of Carpenter's desk; each caught up in their own emotions about what they were soon to learn.

'Sarah, the first thing we need to talk about is quite personal, and I need to ask if you want to hear this alone. Would you like Suzie and her mother to leave?' he asked kindly.

Sarah shook her head. 'Without them, we wouldn't be here at all. They can stay.'

He nodded and continued. 'Well, then, let's get straight into it. An autopsy has confirmed that it was Louise who we found in the woods.'

A small moan escaped Sarah. Though they had all known it was coming, hearing it loud made it seem all the more real.

'That's not all,' Carpenter carried on, looking a little uncomfortable though maintaining his air of professionalism. 'Under Louise's fingernails, we found traces of skin. After performing DNA tests, we can confirm that this skin belongs to your ex-partner – Andrew.'

He put the report down and looked at them all. 'If we can find a witness to confirm that Louise was in the area on the night that we believe she was killed, then we've got him.'

Suzie's mind was racing, pulling at the strings of her memory until suddenly she got a hit. 'What about his girlfriend? I saw her with him at the pub. Maybe he said something to her, or she saw something...?'

Carpenter was nodding. 'That's an avenue we are already exploring.'

Across the room, Sarah was a mess – her tears overwhelming her once again. Glancing across, Carpenter beckoned Brian to lean closer, adding, 'Perhaps you should take Sarah home now. She needs rest. A doctor should be able to prescribe something.'

Brian nodded and stood, placing a hand under Sarah's arm and lifting her to her feet from her chair. 'May I suggest as well,' Carpenter added, looking directly at Sarah, 'that you see a counsellor? Nobody should go through this without proper support.'

'I want to speak to him,' Sarah whispered in a shaky voice. Carpenter nodded. 'Yes, often the family wants to speak to the individual responsible for their pain. And your chance will come. But first, we need to finish this and bring him in. Don't go through this alone, Sarah,' Carpenter finished solemnly.

Suzie and Jill sat watching the interaction, overwhelmed with their own emotions of shock and terrible, terrible sadness. Suddenly, taking them all by surprise, Suzie stood and walked over, crouching beside Sarah, who was now on the floor leaning back against a wall, her knees bent and her head in her arms sobbing. Looking up, Suzie asked to speak to Sarah alone. She didn't have to ask twice.

Suzie put her arms around Sarah and pulled her into an embrace before feeling around in her pocket for the bracelet she had found earlier that day. 'Sarah… do you recognise this?'

Sarah, clasping her hands around the bracelet, looked up at Suzie with a watery smile. 'This belonged to Louise's godmother. She always said she wanted Louise to have it one day – to wear on her own wedding day.'

She turned away. 'Annie died of cancer not too long ago. Louise was heartbroken. They had been so close. How did you find it?' she asked suddenly, as if only just realising what was happening.

'I think we should get some fresh air,' Suzie replied, standing up. Sarah, nodding, stood up beside her. They made their way out of Carpenters office and headed back down the corridor, out into the open park area which sat behind the police station. Suzie couldn't see her mum or Brian and figured they must have gone to the coffee machine in the station or were with Carpenter somewhere.

As they sat down on a bench overlooking the children's playground, Suzie explained what had happened earlier that day in the charity shop – how the woman had spoken to her and kissed her cheek. How she had looked exactly like the woman her gran had described days before.

As she finished, she looked over at Sarah and was surprised to see a smile on the woman's face. 'She always said she would look after my Louise,' she said softly. 'Good old Annie, making good on her word – like always.' She hugged Suzie then and kissed her on the cheek – just like Annie had done.

'I can't thank you enough, Suzie,' she said.

'Promise me you'll speak to someone, like Superintendent Carpenter said,' Suzie said, a frown etched on her face. 'You can't go through this alone, Sarah.'

The woman nodded. It was enough.

As Suzie and Sarah got up from the bench, their arms locked together, a sense of peace fell over them both.

Brian and Jill were stood by the car waiting for them as they returned. Nobody spoke – really, nobody needed to.

As they dropped Jill and Suzie back at Rose's house, Sarah got out and gave both Suzie and Jill a big hug.

'Thank you,' she whispered, not just to Suzie but to Jill as well. The woman who had been a rock for all of them and who had allowed her daughter to put herself at risk for the truth.

'Can I ask just one more thing?' Suzie said to Sarah as they pulled apart. 'Can you tell me when Louise's funeral will be? If it's okay with you, I would like to come and show my respects. I know I didn't know Louise, but I know I would have liked her.'

Sarah hugged Suzie again. 'Without a doubt, Suzie, I would love you to come. You remind me of Louise. I think you would have been great friends. And Suzie, your gift, whatever it is and however it came to find you, is good. Use it for good.'

All Jill could do was watch on, letting her daughter have this moment with the mother of the girl she had found. She felt full of pride.

Brian and Sarah eventually drove off, and Jill and Suzie went back into the house, totally drained. They would never be able to forget the last few weeks, and though they both wished things could have ended differently for Louise and her family, Suzie felt privileged that she had been the one to help. It was a monumental responsibility, but one she knew she could use well – if she wanted to.

Jill, meanwhile, didn't feel the need to ask Suzie what had been said between her and Sarah. She knew that if Suzie wanted to talk, she would.

And so the two of them, arm in arm, stepped through the house and back into the garden, where Melissa and Rose were waiting to hear everything that had happened.

It was over.

35

Two days later, as Melissa and Suzie were packing to head home the following morning, the phone rang. Thinking nothing of it, the girls continued chatting and packing their things until Jill's voice called up the stairs.

'Suzie? Brian's on the phone, him and Sarah want to pop round before we leave tomorrow.'

Dashing to the top of the stairs to nod her head in enthusiastic agreement, Suzie grabbed Melissa's hand as the two of them made their way downstairs. Just as the girls arrived in the hall, the doorbell rang. That was quick, thought Suzie as she pulled the door open – but it wasn't Brian or Sarah on the doorstep.

'Hello, Suzie,' rumbled the deep voice of Superintendent Carpenter. Taken aback, Suzie gazed at him for a split second before standing back and opening the door wider to let him through whilst telling him that Brian and Sarah were on their way over. He just nodded.

As they all seated themselves in the living room, Carpenter wasted no time on niceties. 'We charged Andrew this morning on a count of murder,' he said abruptly, launching straight into the reason he had come. He saw no point in beating around the bush and smiled at them all. 'I imagine that's what Brian and Sarah want to tell you. I must say, I'm glad I got to tell you first.'

Suzie's breath, which she hadn't realised she had been holding, suddenly escaped her in a massive sigh of relief. She hadn't thought she was concerned about the outcome, but now she knew. She realised she had been waiting with bated breath to hear if justice for Louise would come.

Tuning back in, she heard Carpenter explain how the DNA under Louise's fingernails, small pieces of skin that had been scratched from Andy's arms and face, had shown signs of a significant struggle. The rug had clinched the deal, with Sarah providing photographic evidence of the rug in the house, which exactly matched that found in the woods.

Just as he stood to leave, Carpenter faced Suzie and thanked her for all she had done – not just assisting the investigation but showing true bravery in communicating her visions and doing, what he termed, the 'right thing.'

'You know, when you first came into the station, I was ready to take everything you said with a pinch of salt. Until then, all we had were false leads and spiritualists, and I truly thought you might well be the same, a time waster. But seeing how everything fit together, what you were saying, and the fact both Sarah and Brian seemed to be wholly behind you... I put faith in myself to take a chance, and I am so glad I did.'

And with that, he finished his coffee, thanked the family, and saw himself out.

Not long after he had left, the doorbell rang again. The door opened to reveal Brian and Sarah – Sarah looking better than they had ever seen her, as if a weight had been lifted from her shoulders. 'You heard?' she asked by way of greeting.

Suzie nodded, and Sarah fell into her arms, pulling her close. 'Thank you,' she said into Suzie's hair.

Suzie wasn't sure how many more times she could hear those two little words, but she didn't say anything.

As they pulled apart, Brian spoke. 'We just wanted to say goodbye to you both, and to your grandma and your friend, Melissa. Without you – all of you – we wouldn't be here today. Louise's funeral is to be next Friday, and we would like it if you could all come.'

He glanced around at them all, nodding curtly at their warm smiles.

The funeral was to take place at the local cemetery just behind the park perched atop a small hill.

After confirming the details, times and other arrangements, Jill said they would get the train down together to attend.

And then, for the first time since they had met, they all simply enjoyed each other's company – Sarah sharing stories from Louise's childhood, Brian telling them all about some of the individuals who had tried and failed to contact Louise's spirit. The conversation soon turned to Suzie and Melissa and their plans for the following year. While Melissa excitedly shared ideas for her trip and travels, Suzie stayed quiet – still unsure of the road her life was to take.

Did this gift of hers change anything?

36

The next morning, after a final evening of Grandma's cooking and more than one bottle of wine, the four of them headed to the train station – the start of this journey and the place where it all first changed.

Suzie and Melissa were looking forward to getting home and catching up with their friends; Melissa also realising how much she had missed her family. She couldn't wait to see them. They had a lot to catch up on.

As they boarded the train, Suzie and Melissa decided on one thing – and that was to keep everything quiet – for now.

After the three-hour journey, they arrived back in Leeds, welcomed by clouds and a distinctly chilly breeze in the air. Ah, the North.

They jumped in a taxi and pulled up outside their home within fifteen minutes, after a quick detour to drop Melissa off at home. Jill and Suzie unpacked their clothes before Jill dashed out to pick up a takeaway – preferring the comfort of a Chinese to the idea of cooking themselves.

'You know, Mum...' Suzie started as they dug into the Chinese. 'You're always there for me... I can't imagine how Sarah is going to cope without Louise. I think they had the same relationship we have.'

'Yes, love, I think you're right,' Jill agreed, nudging her daughter's arm. Then, dropping her fork, she suddenly scooted around the table and pulled Suzie into a huge hug. It was a moment both of them would share for the rest of their lives, no matter how Suzie's life was now going to change – because she knew it would. If not that night or the next day, it was certainly going to change.

One thing Suzie did know, despite all her uncertainty and doubt, was that she was glad she had been there to help Sarah. She also knew, in that moment, that she wanted to be there for other families. If she had been given this gift, then it was for a reason, and that was something she had to deal with herself.

37

The following week, Suzie, Jill and Melissa boarded the train for Essex, deciding to head straight to the church where they would meet Rose before the service.

As it had been all summer, it was a lovely warm day, and as everyone started to arrive, they noticed that every single person was wearing something bright; as requested by Sarah. It truly was a sight to see.

Suzie had chosen a yellow silk blouse paired with black trousers and yellow shoes – the very shoes she had found at a charity shop just that week. Melissa was wearing a vibrant blue blouse, also paired with black trousers and black shoes, while Jill had opted for a more reserved look; a pink camisole top, white trousers and white shoes. A delicate but very pretty look.

Louise was to be cremated. Although Sarah would have liked to have somewhere to go and visit her daughter, she was also aware that on the odd occasions when both herself and Louise had been watching anything on television involving funerals, Louise had taken the time to comment on how she would like to be cremated; her ashes taken to somewhere beautiful and hot, with lovely views and plenty of ocean.

Sarah had always just smiled at her daughter during those conversations, thinking to herself how she certainly wouldn't be around to make that decision for Louise. How wrong she'd been.

Despite following Louise's wishes, she still didn't know where she would take her for her final resting place. But wherever it was, she would make sure it had the most beautiful view in the world.

It was a lovely ceremony. Brian gave a remarkable speech about Louise, as there was no way Sarah could even consider doing it herself – but Brian did a fantastic job. One of Louise's aunts from her father's side also stood up and talked about her; not one dry eye left by the time she had finished.

After the ceremony, full of tears and laughter and Louise's favourite songs, they all went back to Sarah's house, joining the caterers who Brian had booked to do sandwiches and cakes. But nobody felt like eating – the air was too full of sadness.

Just as Jill was considering rounding her mum and the girls up to leave, a man stood up and started talking. His voice was quiet at first, a little wobbly as he told a story from Louise's younger days. But as he continued, and more and more people gathered round to listen, his voice grew louder, more confident, and soon the atmosphere became one of celebration. Celebrating a life that had been full, lively, and full of joy.

By the time Jill, Rose, Suzie, Melissa were ready to leave, the dark house had become a brighter home. No doubt the pain would hit Sarah again later, but Uncle Mikey – as the crowd had come to know him – had made a real difference.

The girls said their goodbyes to the guests, and Suzie had a few moments alone with Sarah. Theirs was now a relationship that would run and run – there was no doubt about it.

38

Reminiscing wasn't all that Sarah and Suzie had spoken about in their final moments before Jill, Suzie and Melissa headed back with Rose for the night before heading off back to Leeds the next day.

Suzie wanted to tell Sarah about the magpie's constant appearance at the most difficult times and so Suzie had decided in her few moments with Sarah to tell her the help that had come from an unlikely source.

The magpie which, Suzie now knew, had been sent by Louise – in one way or another – to guide her towards the final truth.

When Sarah had listened to what Suzie had to say one final time, she didn't feel sad. Instead, she felt at peace – knowing now, at last, that Suzie had been doing her daughter's bidding from the start.

She also knew that she would never look at a magpie in the same way again.

One for sorrow, that was for sure. But with a companion nearby, perhaps her life could start to attract some joy as well – from memories and stories.

39

By the time they arrived back in Leeds the next day, they were all shattered. It had truly been one hell of a journey.

Melissa was staying at Suzie's house, with plans for the two of them to catch up with their group of friends the following evening. Suzie found she was really looking forward to it – craving some activity outside of the drama of the last few weeks and excited to spend time with people who didn't know all about her visions and nightmares.

◉◉◉

The weather up North was a little cooler than it had been in Essex, and Suzie and Melissa headed to the high street the next morning to seek out a few new outfit choices for their night ahead. When they left Essex, Rose had given both Suzie and Melissa £50 to treat themselves. Suzie wasn't sure if she felt guilty that everything had happened under her roof, but she hoped not. Both she and Melissa had enjoyed their time in Essex, despite all the upheaval and uncertainty, and had particularly enjoyed spending time with Suzie's gran.

Melissa had been particularly chuffed to have been recognised as well, and Suzie knew from the glow in her eyes

195

as she handed over the £50 in exchange for a new dress and heels that the gift from her Gran had meant a lot more than just cash. Melissa was part of her family.

'I feel so much more sophisticated and grown up now,' said Melissa laughing, as they ordered pizza and a glass of wine in a small Italian at the quiet end of the high street.

'Better not drink too much,' warned Suzie, as she too ordered a small glass of wine. 'We don't want to embarrass ourselves!'

The girls had both chosen short, simple dresses which accentuated their figures, similar styles but each with their own design. Melissa had opted for a vibrant green, while Suzie stuck to a block print of black and white.

When they were finished with their pizza and had drained their wine glasses, the two of them headed back to Suzie's to get ready, and to spend some time with Jill before going out.

'You will both look stunning tonight,' commented Jill when the two had returned and were parading their new clothes in front of Suzie's mum. 'If you don't find handsome new boyfriends tonight, then there is something very wrong with the water.'

Suzie laughed out loud. 'First of all, that is such an old saying mum, secondly, you must be joking. I mean, have you seen the talent we have round here? Please.' She rolled her eyes at Melissa.

Jill just gave her a knowing smile and persisted. 'You know what, Suzie? I don't care what you think now – when you see somebody who is right, love will blossom.'

Suzie was mortified and hurriedly tried to usher Melissa out of the room.

'Oh, Mum, please stop now! You sound like something from a Jane Austen book.' Jill laughed at their retreating backs.

Later, as the three of them ate dinner together, Jill asked, 'I thought you were meeting your friends tonight?'

'Yes, we are,' Suzie nodded. 'But we're not meeting them until 9ish, then we're all going on to Max's house. His mum and dad are away, so a few of us are going round to his. Sorry, Mum. Thought I'd told you.'

'No love, you didn't. It doesn't matter. I'll come and collect you when you're done.'

'No, it's okay, Mum. I mean, what if we stay until, like, three in the morning?' She laughed, but Jill shook her head.

'It doesn't matter, love, not after what we've been through the last few weeks.'

Suddenly Suzie realised what she meant.

'Oh, Mum, it was somebody she knew! Not a stranger on the streets. If it makes you feel better, we'll get a taxi,' she added. Melissa nodded in agreement.

'What about we stay all night and come home tomorrow morning? We are nearly nineteen, Mum. We'll be fine.' She put a hand on her mum's arm and gave her a quick kiss of reassurance.

'Ok, I know. Well, make sure you both have your mobiles on.'

Finishing their dinner, both girls left the table smiling at Jill for her last comment and headed upstairs to get ready.

A couple of hours later, Suzie and Melissa said their goodbyes to Jill and headed towards the local pub.

When they arrived, some of the group were already there. Nige – everybody shortened Nigel's name – Max and Simon. Ordering the first round of drinks, the group was soon laughing and joking like no time had passed as they waited for the others to arrive.

After a couple of hours in the pub catching up, the rest of the group joining them in dribs and drabs over the next hour; they headed back to Max's house. It was there that Suzie and Melissa told them all about what happened in Essex – explaining why they hadn't really been in contact, and why everything had been so weird for them lately.

Jill had asked Suzie earlier that day if she planned on telling her friends, and as she thought about it, she realised she wanted to. They were her friends, and she trusted them not to say anything to anyone. Plus, Suzie found that just the act of telling them took a load off her shoulders – even if she was a little tipsy by the time she did it.

'So, do you mean you can look into the future, Suzie?' asked Nige as he munched on a slice of pizza in Max's basement den some hours later.

Suzie laughed. 'I knew you wouldn't understand what I was trying to tell you. No, I can't, I can't read your minds, I certainly can't read lottery numbers for you, and I promise I won't start any weird voodoo stuff or anything. I know it's weird... it's more of a physical thing. Like, I only felt what was happening when I wore Louise's clothes.' She shrugged.

'So then, say I die next week, and you wore my boxers. Would you be able to tell the police what happened to me?' he persisted, nudging the others around the table.

'Right, that's enough now,' said Melissa. She knew Suzie could handle the questions, and while her face was still somewhat amused, the stupid questions were getting a little boring.

'Sorry, Suze, I'll give it up. I do believe you. It's just I wish I'd been there to see it all! It sounds great,' added Nige.

'Well, believe me, it wasn't great. All that's good is that the guy is now going to trial... but to have murdered a young girl... A girl my age as well. She could have been any one of us here.' Suzie looked around at the group, who sat soberly watching her.

After a moment's silence, Chalkie began to speak.

'Hey, you know what we should do while your mum and dad are away, Max? We should set up a Ouija board and see what happens.'

'Leave it,' said Suzie quietly. 'You don't want to mess with things you don't understand.'

'Hear, hear,' agreed Max, giving her a smile of support.

Again, the conversation dried up, and they sat quietly for a few moments. But Chalkie wasn't letting it go.

'Oh, come on, are you scared, Max? What else are we going to do?'

'No, not scared,' laughed Max. 'If you really want to do it, then fine. Suzie, you don't have to stay. There's a spare room upstairs if you want, or I can order a taxi for you?' He was keen not to upset her.

But Suzie realised they were just looking for some fun. What the hell, hey?

'I warn you though, things are different now. You don't want to mess in dangerous things you don't understand,' she said as they gathered what they needed and drew chairs around a table.

Though she didn't mind watching, she didn't want to join in and so decided to sit out – Melissa joining her on the sofa on the other side of the den.

They watched on as the rest of their friends got a tall glass and put it on the table, their fingers resting on the top of the glass. It was Chalkie who made the first move.

Suzie had asked them not to do a proper Ouija board. While the glass movement made her nervous, it wasn't as bad as it could be.

'Is anybody there?' asked Chalkie playfully.

Nothing happened.

'Is anybody there? Please, if anybody is here in the spirit world, please move the glass.'

No movement.

'If anybody is here, move the glass for yes and stay still for no.'

At that, the glass made a slight movement to the left of the table. As the group watched on, it didn't stop until it came to the end of the table and nearly fell off. A few of them smirked, not believing it. One of them must have done it.

The guys moved the glass back into the centre of the table again, deciding that Chalkie had brought them this far and so he should do all the talking.

'Are you male?' Again, the glass moved. This time, there were no smiles. None of them had moved it.

Or had they...?

The author

Jodie A. Samuel was born in Morley, Leeds, in 1967. Jodie is a proud mother of two children and a grandmother to Amelia and Louie. She cherishes her family and loves spending quality time with them, especially with her little grandchildren. Despite having a successful career as a litigator, Jodie's true passion lies in writing. Jodie finds writing to be a therapeutic and creative outlet, allowing her to express herself and explore new ideas. Jodie is also an animal lover and shares her home with two furry companions. Her mischievous cocker spaniel, Penny, keeps her on her toes and provides endless entertainment with her antics. Meanwhile, her elderly fluffy black cat, Belle, is a quiet and calming presence in her home. Jodie is currently working on her second novel. Her latest project revolves around the character Suzie and her next chapter.